THE SCENT OF HEATHER

Maggie and her sister Rebecca come to Heather House to recover from the drowning deaths of their two husbands. But the house seems to be haunted by the ghost of its one-time owner, Heather Lambert, the scent of the eponymous herb occasionally drifting through the air. As Maggie falls under the spell of the house, events take a more sinister turn when she narrowly survives an attempt on her life, and then the housekeeper is found murdered . . . Can Maggie discover the secret of Heather House before it's too late?

V. J. BANIS

THE SCENT OF HEATHER

Complete and Unabridged

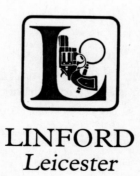

LINFORD
Leicester

First published in Great Britain

First Linford Edition
published 2015

A catalogue record for this book is available
from the British Library.

ISBN 978–1–4448–2518–3

Published by
F. A. Thorpe (Publishing)
Anstey, Leicestershire

Set by Words & Graphics Ltd.
Anstey, Leicestershire
Printed and bound in Great Britain by
T. J. International Ltd., Padstow, Cornwall

This book is printed on acid-free paper

1

People believed Maggie Garrison loved her sister very much. They were wrong, but Maggie would never admit it, not even to herself. Ever since Rebecca was born they'd been inseparable, apart only long enough to enjoy short honeymoons with their respective husbands. They lived in adjoining apartments. They shared the common fate of childless marriages. They even shared a common sorrow when their husbands drowned while together on a fishing excursion.

But were the two men really dead? The bodies were never recovered. Although the insurance company was convinced that they were dead, Maggie continued to have her doubts.

There was something in the way her sister had accepted the news of their husbands' deaths that made Maggie leery. Rebecca had accepted her loss so easily, but Rebecca accepted everything easily.

* * *

They had been driving for hours. When the large, rambling house loomed up before them, Maggie tucked her knitting back into her bag and said, 'Ah, at last. I thought we were going to have to drive off the end of the earth before getting here.'

'Gloomy-looking place, isn't it?' Rebecca said as she slowed the car and turned into the driveway.

'That's what the real-estate man meant when he said the place had character.'

'That must be his car parked under the portico.'

As Rebecca steered the Mercedes up the driveway a man got out of the parked car and waved. Rebecca pulled to a stop directly behind his sedan and leaned toward Maggie, eyeing the man standing in the driveway. 'Now that's what I call a good-looking hunk of man,' she said softly.

David McCloud walked toward them. He smiled at Rebecca and she felt a delicious little shiver run down her spine. David McCloud was rugged and square-jawed, with romantic blue eyes and hair the color of burnished straw. His features were chiseled, the mouth full and sensuous. He was tall, well over six feet, with the physique of an athlete.

'Hi,' he said. 'I'm David McCloud.' His voice was a beautiful complement to the rest of him. 'You must be Mrs. Garrison and Mrs. Shepard.'

Rebecca extended her hand. 'I'm Rebecca Shepard. This is my sister, Maggie Garrison.'

Maggie, too, felt a little shiver shoot through her when she shook hands with him. Rebecca was right, he was extremely good-looking.

'Well, here's the house I leased for you. I hope you'll like it,' David said. 'It's pretty large, as you may have surmised from the pictures I sent you, and the grounds go on forever.'

The three of them walked along a path leading off the driveway. There was a large, open patio completely surrounded on three sides by a horseshoe-shaped Spanish *hacienda* with a clay-tiled roof painted dusty rose. There were little cactus gardens spotted here and there, rocks, flaming hibiscus and droopy shade trees. A large, cup-shaped cactus dominated one corner of the garden; yucca stretched tall in clusters of bell-shaped flowers on tall stems; tiny rock plants forced their way between the neatly arranged rocks, spilling their lovely butter-yellow flowers against their surroundings. Avocado trees were strategically placed to give shade where it was needed. The rambling garden looked like a quiet refuge from a world of turmoil.

'It's heavenly,' Maggie said, visibly enchanted.

'Sophie takes pride in the patio. She spends all her time keeping it tidy.'

'Sophie? Who's Sophie?' inquired Maggie.

'She comes with the place. When you lease Heather House you automatically get Sophie in the bargain. She's a strange little thing . . . not quite right in the head, but harmless as a fly.'

Rebecca arched an eyebrow. 'Some flies are lethal.'

David smiled and shook his head. 'Not Sophie. She's just a child mentally, and as hard a worker as you'll find. She used to work for the Lamberts — they're the

4

owners — and according to Sophie's way of thinking, she still works for them.'

'Oh, yes,' Maggie said. 'You mentioned the Lamberts in your letter.'

'Mr. Lambert disappeared some twenty years ago. His wife, Heather, died about a year or two ago.' David looked up at the house. 'The place is in real good shape but I'm afraid the fields around it have fallen into wasteland now, with the exception of this garden, of course.'

Rebecca glanced back over her shoulder at the neglected land. 'Just so long as there is plenty of privacy, that's all we're concerned about.'

'There's plenty of that, have no fears,' David assured her. 'Shall we have a look inside?'

Maggie's eye wandered to a strange square tower tucked onto the westerly corner. It seemed out of character with the rest of the house. David followed her glance.

'It was built after Mr. Lambert disappeared,' he told her, nodding at the structure. 'Heather Lambert used it as a watchtower, I understand. She died up there, sitting at that window.'

Maggie shivered and looked away.

'Watchtower?' Rebecca said.

'Yes,' David said. 'She suspected that her husband had run off with another woman. She never gave up hope that he'd return to her. I hope you don't pay too much attention to Sophie; she is convinced that Heather Lambert is still up there, waiting.'

Rebecca laughed. 'Great. I've always wanted to live in a haunted house.'

Haunted house. The remark suddenly triggered something deep down inside Maggie. A tiny frown creased her brow. As she walked toward Heather House the place seemed to wrap itself around her . . . like a giant spider web.

David followed Maggie and Rebecca into the house. They found themselves in a large tiled foyer with a wrought-iron staircase sweeping up to the second floor. On their left, two steps below the foyer, was an immense living room with a beamed ceiling and large, arched doorways and stately casement windows. The heavy furniture, wood, leather and velvet, was very much in the Spanish style.

'I'm impressed,' Maggie said. 'Who did you say lived here? Carlotta and Maximilian? I must say, it's rather grand.'

'This is the single-level wing,' David explained as he crossed the living room. 'It includes this room, the library over there and several bedrooms through here.' He pointed to a set of double doors with heavily carved moldings. 'On the other side of the foyer is the split-level part of the house. On its lower level there's a formal dining room, breakfast room, kitchen, pantry, laundry room and servants' quarters. The upstairs rooms need not be used at all if you don't want to bother with them. You could live very comfortably on just this ground floor.'

'Oh, but I want to see everything,' Maggie said. 'If this room is any indication, I'm sure I'll love every inch of the place.'

David showed them the library, which was stacked with shelves of books.

'Old Mr. Lambert must have been quite a scholar,' Maggie noted, running her fingers across the spines of books on philosophy, political science, religion, music, painting, archaeology and ancient and modern history.

David laughed. 'These belonged to Heather Lambert, I understand,' he said, nodding toward the bookcases. 'From what I hear, Mr. Lambert's only interest was beautiful women.' He smiled broadly, glancing from Rebecca to Maggie and back to Rebecca. 'Of course, I can't say that I blame him. I'm afraid I'm afflicted with that vice myself.'

Rebecca cocked her head at him and gave him a seductive smile. 'Are you married, Mr. McCloud?'

'Rebecca!' Maggie said, startled.

David laughed. 'No. I'm still a bachelor.'

'Why?' Rebecca asked boldly.

Maggie gave her an admonishing look. 'Really, Rebecca. You're being terribly forward.' She looked at David. 'You must excuse my sister, Mr. McCloud. She sometimes says things without thinking how tactless they are.'

Again David laughed. 'I don't mind, Mrs. Garrison.' He looked at Rebecca. 'I guess I just never found the right woman.

I'm still looking, however.'

'Me, too,' Rebecca said boldly.

'I assume then that you're divorced.'

'We're widows . . . both of us. Our husbands went out fishing together and their boat capsized. They drowned.'

'I'm sorry.'

'Don't be,' Rebecca said, giving her hair a flip. 'If George hadn't died I would have divorced him anyway.'

Maggie stiffened. 'Rebecca,' she said with ice dripping from her tongue, 'I think you're being most disrespectful and horribly brazen. I insist you behave yourself.'

'Oh, pooh,' Rebecca scoffed. 'I'm just being truthful. I'd rather be that than a hypocrite.'

'Come on,' David said, 'I'll show you the rest of the place.'

From the library they went through several other rooms that were furnished as guest bedrooms, complete with their own private bathrooms. The rooms were all large and cool and airy with huge windows, tall beamed ceilings and tiled floors on which deep shag rugs were

9

scattered. Most of the rooms had French doors that opened out onto the inner-court patio.

'Simply charming,' Maggie said. 'I adore it.'

The other wing contained a large, impressive dining room of massive proportions, a more intimate breakfast room painted a drab green, a paneled pantry, a gigantic kitchen, a laundry room and servants' rooms.

Upstairs the rooms were even larger and more elegant. Maggie fell hopelessly in love with the larger bedroom at the top of the stairs.

'It's bigger than my entire old apartment,' Maggie said as she stepped up onto the platform that held a mammoth four-poster bed with brocade trappings. 'Oh, I've just got to sleep here. It is absolutely beautiful.'

'This was Heather Lambert's bedroom, I understand,' David said. 'It hasn't been used for a few years, so please excuse the dust.'

Maggie frowned. 'But I thought you said this Sophie woman thinks her mistress is still alive. Wouldn't Mrs. Lambert's bedroom be her prime concern?'

'Heather Lambert didn't use this room after her husband disappeared. She lived almost entirely in the tower. She hardly ever came down, they say.'

Maggie sat down and tested the bed. 'Well, what do you think, Rebecca?'

Rebecca tilted up her chin. 'What do I think? Since when have you asked for my advice about anything? You're the big sister. Everybody has to do what their big sister tells them, don't they?' She knew she was being spiteful but she couldn't help it. She felt she had to get back at Maggie somehow for the way she had admonished her in front of David.

Maggie chose to ignore the frost in her sister's voice. 'When can we move in?' she asked.

David smiled. 'Will tomorrow be soon enough?'

'Tomorrow? Why not today?' Maggie asked.

'I really would like Sophie to give this room a real good cleaning now that I know you'll be sleeping here. Besides, I doubt if there are any provisions in the house. The cupboards are pretty bare, I'm afraid.'

'Rebecca and I can take care of that in no time flat,' Maggie said. 'And I'll have this room shipshape in no time at all.'

David opened his mouth to object but Rebecca stepped in with, 'Don't argue with her highness, Mr. McCloud. You'll only be fighting a losing battle. Maggie always gets her own way about everything.'

David saw the friction spark between them. 'I'm sorry, Mrs. Garrison,' he said, 'but moving in today would be quite impossible. There are no utilities turned on in the house as yet.'

Maggie's eyes widened. 'No utilities? But I thought you said this Sophie person has been living here keeping the place up.'

'That's true enough, but I'm afraid we're very frugal here in Pinebrook. As the manager of the place I've tried to keep expenses at a minimum until we had a paying tenant.'

'I see. Well, in that case, I suppose tomorrow will have to do.'

'Do you mean to tell me that you made

12

the housekeeper live here without any water or electricity?' Rebecca asked.

David looked uncomfortable. 'Old Sophie's used to it. There's water, of course, and gas, but the electricity is off.'

'How does she manage?' Rebecca persisted.

'She hasn't complained. She likes kerosene lamps, I guess. Speaking of Sophie, I should go find her and introduce her to you. She's around somewhere.' He turned and left the room quickly.

Maggie shook her head. 'Dashing Dave seems to have a miserly streak underneath all that charm and beauty.'

As much as Rebecca wanted to agree, she didn't. She was still annoyed with Maggie. 'This place must cost a fortune to keep up. He's just being sensible. He's a businessman, after all.'

Maggie had the feeling that Rebecca was looking for an argument. She wouldn't argue. There'd been too much of that recently. She merely shrugged, turned and walked out of the room. Rebecca hesitated for a moment, then followed her sister.

They found David McCloud in the

living room talking to a frail-looking woman in a shapeless housedress.

'This is Sophie,' David said. He leaned close to Sophie and, as if talking to a child, said, 'Sophie, this is Mrs. Garrison and this is Mrs. Shepard.'

'How do you do,' Sophie mumbled and made a quick little curtsy. She was a woman well into her middle years, but there was something about her that made her seem more girl than woman. She was frail, almost tiny, with arms like matchsticks, and shoulders so bony the dress she wore seemed as if it were draping a skeleton. Her eyes were bright, but the mouth lacked personality and the face was nothing more than a blank expanse. She took refuge behind David, and stared around him at Maggie most queerly.

'Sophie's terribly shy, I'm afraid,' David explained, 'but an excellent worker. She'll be all right after she gets used to you and you to her.' He glanced around at the girl. 'Mrs. Garrison and Mrs. Shepard will be living here, Sophie. I want you to take real good care of them. Do you understand?'

'Living here?' Sophie mumbled. She

14

did not seem to grasp what David had said. 'Miss Heather . . . '

'It's all right,' David said quickly, cutting Sophie off. 'These ladies will live here and you will work for them now.'

Sophie's big eyes looked up into David's face and gave a quick little shake of her head. She gazed at Maggie, then at Rebecca. The ladies smiled indulgently. Sophie just stared at them. Then she darted out from behind David and rushed out of the room.

'She takes some getting used to,' David said softly, 'but I'm sure you will be quite satisfied with her.'

'While I'm here,' Maggie said, starting in the direction in which Sophie had fled, 'I think I'll check the kitchen supplies and make up a shopping list. It'll give Sophie a chance to get to know me and vice versa.'

David glanced after Maggie and then turned to Rebecca. He lowered his voice. 'You and your sister will love it here,' he said.

'Maggie might, but I'm not all that sure about myself.' Rebecca glanced around.

'Oh, it's okay as far as houses go. But houses never meant much to me. Right now I'm more attracted to things like penthouses and the excitement of city life.'

'Then why in heaven's name did you agree to come to Pinebrook to lease a house?' He fumbled in his jacket pocket for a cigarette. He shook one out of the pack and offered it to Rebecca.

'Thanks.' She strolled toward one of the windows that overlooked the garden. David moved to stand beside her. He lit her cigarette.

'It was really my idea, believe it or not. Losing our husbands was quite a surprise — both of them at once like that. Maggie really took it hard. As I told you, I wasn't all that broken up about losing George. Naturally I didn't want to see him dead, but as long as that was the way it happened, I accepted it readily enough. Maggie, though, started to mope around. You've seen what she's like — all that mourning black, the long face, the whole bit. I suggested we get out of the city for a while and find some quiet little corner until she worked herself out of her depression. I thought if I got Maggie away from everything that reminded her of her husband she'd come out of her shell and turn back into being a woman.'

'I think she's a very attractive woman,' David said.

Rebecca nodded. 'Yes, under those widow's weeds Maggie is quite a looker, but she doesn't think she is. She has this thing about feeling sorry for herself and she expects everyone else to feel that way about her, too.'

'You must be very fond of your sister to sacrifice your own happiness for her sake.'

'Oh, I wouldn't go as far as to say that. I know I'm being foolish to live my life to suit Maggie — at least for the time being — but, you see, Maggie more or less raised me from the time I was a child. So I'm kind of indebted to her, if you know what I mean.'

'You should never try to live your life for someone else,' David said. 'It usually ends up by making everybody concerned unhappy.'

Maggie came back into the room. David turned to her. 'Well, Mrs. Garrison, did

17

everything go all right between you and Sophie?'

'You're right, Mr. McCloud. She's a bit shy and more than just a bit odd, but I think we communicated.'

'As I told you, she isn't completely right upstairs,' David said, tapping his temple. 'But she's very sweet. A good worker, honest, dependable, and a fantastic cook.'

'Oh, I'm sure we'll get along just fine,' Maggie said. 'The only disconcerting thing about her is that she kept calling me Miss Heather.'

'Well, Miss Heather,' Rebecca said pointedly, 'shall we follow Mr. McCloud back into Pinebrook and find ourselves a place for the night? I don't want to stay here. I'm afraid of the dark.'

David laughed. 'I'm afraid there isn't any hotel in Pinebrook, but we have a nice little rooming house. It's small but I think Mrs. Johnston, the owner, will make you comfortable.'

'Do you live in Pinebrook, Mr. McCloud, or do you commute?' Rebecca asked.

'I own a little place up in the mountains near here but I only go there on weekends

18

or whenever I want to get away from things. During the week I rent a couple of rooms — like a small apartment — from Mrs. Johnston.'

'Then we'll be neighbors, at least for tonight,' Rebecca said.

'That we will.' He gave Rebecca a wink, which Maggie did not see.

2

Mrs. Johnston was as nondescript-looking as her house. She wore a long white skirt, white blouse and apron and looked more like a hospital attendant than an innkeeper. Her hair was dyed pale blonde. She was tall and thin, and her eyes were cool, almost cold. Maggie introduced herself and Rebecca.

'Yes,' Mrs. Johnston said without smiling, 'Mr. McCloud telephoned.' Her voice was pleasant enough and showed a kind of refinement. 'I've been expecting you. This way, please.' She turned sharply and started along a hallway that ended at a flight of stairs. She marched rather than walked up the stairway with Maggie and Rebecca close behind.

'In here,' Mrs. Johnston said, pushing open a door. 'I don't serve meals. The room will be eighteen dollars for the night.'

'Thank you, it will do nicely,' Maggie said as she looked at the barren little white room. It was so bleached out it was depressing, but Maggie reminded herself that there was no other place to stay. 'We'll only be staying for tonight. We've leased the Lambert place and plan on moving in tomorrow.'

Maggie saw the woman's eyes widen and her chin drop but Mrs. Johnston — although obviously surprised at the news — made no sound. In a moment she regained her composure. She crossed her arms tightly as though hugging back any comment she was tempted to make. 'I see,' she said as she straightened herself up to her full height. Saying no more, she pivoted and left Maggie and Rebecca alone.

Maggie went to the door and closed it. 'She certainly is a bundle of charm.'

Rebecca looked around the room. 'You can easily tell she had a hand in decorating this place. I've seen the inside of refrigerators that were cozier than this.'

Maggie laughed, forgetting the friction between them, 'Yes, it could use a bit of color. Mrs. Johnston obviously has a white-fetish.' She sighed and put her overnight case on the bed, unsnapping the lid.

'Oh, well, it's only for one night. What do you think of the house we rented, Rebecca?'

'It's okay. A house is a house. It'll do for the time being. It's bigger than I thought it would be.'

'I like it. It is rather large, I must admit, but I think we'll be happy there.' She took out her nightgown and draped it across the coverlet. 'I thought the place had a nice personality, didn't you?'

'How can a house have a personality?'

'Places and things have moods and feelings; haven't you ever felt that?'

'Can't say that I have,' Rebecca answered, sounding totally disinterested in the conversation.

'You will never really appreciate all there is to life, I'm afraid. You're interested only in the superficial, the surface aspects of people and things. You don't take time to look beneath the veneer where the real beauty lies.'

'David mentioned taking us to dinner tonight,' Rebecca said, purposely changing the subject. 'Did he say seven or seven-thirty?'

'Seven. We have time for a nap if you like.'

'I think it's going to be hard enough falling asleep in this white snowdrift at night; I don't think I'd be able to close my eyes in the daylight.' She went toward the door on the opposite wall. 'Good Lord,' she gasped as she saw the all-white bathroom. 'It looks as though somebody dipped this place into a bottle of Clorox. You can hardly tell where the sink and tub are against all this white tile. It's so bright it's giving me a headache.'

Maggie walked over and stood beside her. 'I see what you mean,' she said as she stared at the blinding white bathroom.

'What would possibly induce somebody to go to such extremes over the color white?' Rebecca asked. 'That old gal must be a little loose upstairs.'

Maggie grinned. 'Maybe she has a virgin complex.'

'From the looks of Mrs. Johnston, I doubt if she's aware that women are different from men.' Rebecca crinkled her nose. 'Let's get out of here and take a walk or something. This room is starting to get to me.'

Maggie picked up her purse and

followed Rebecca out of the room. In the hall, Rebecca glanced around. 'One thing about this place does please me, though,' Rebecca said. 'I wonder which are David McCloud's rooms.' She grinned. 'A man like that brightens up even the drabbest places.'

'I marvel at your capacity to get interested in a man as quickly as you do. You know nothing about David McCloud.'

'What's there to know? He wears pants; he has a nice body and a good-looking face.' She chuckled softly. 'You know me, Maggie. I'm a pushover for a handsome man.'

Maggie said nothing. She remembered that night a long, long time ago when she came home unexpectedly and found her husband and Rebecca locked in an embrace. No man was sacred insofar as Rebecca was concerned.

As they opened the front door they bumped into David McCloud. 'Well, where are you two off to?' he asked.

'We're going to see the sights in your town,' Rebecca said.

'Don't get lost. Remember, I'm calling

for you at seven.' He gave a little salute and went past them and up the stairs.

Mrs. Johnston was sweeping the front steps when they came out onto the porch. In her white dress and apron, standing against the white of the building, she was almost invisible. There was a man dozing in a wheelchair at the far end of the porch.

'I trust the room is satisfactory?' Mrs. Johnston asked.

'Fine, fine,' Maggie answered. 'We were just going for a stroll before dinner.'

Mrs. Johnston leaned slightly forward toward Maggie, as though intending to impart a secret. 'You did say you were only staying for tonight, is that correct?'

'Yes,' Maggie answered.

'You'll be moving into Heather House tomorrow?'

'Yes.

'I know it isn't any of my business, Mrs. Garrison, but I believe you are making a mistake by leasing that property.'

'Why do you say that?' Maggie asked, a little taken aback.

'The house is evil,' the woman said. Her eyes went a little wild and she pulled her mouth down at the corners. 'It's a bad place. Go back where you came from.'

Maggie frowned. 'I'm afraid that isn't possible.'

'Don't say I didn't warn you. I wouldn't be found dead in that old place.'

Maggie stiffened. She resented the woman's familiarity. 'I don't think you need worry about being found dead there, Mrs. Johnston,' Maggie said icily. She took a dislike to the woman. 'At least not while my sister and I are living there.' She let the implication rest where it lay.

Mrs. Johnston gave her an ugly little smile. 'You'll be sorry, Mrs. Garrison. You'll live to regret your decision.'

Rebecca, feeling uncomfortable, tugged at Maggie's sleeve. 'Shall we go, Maggie?'

Maggie felt like giving the woman a piece of her mind but she let Rebecca pull her away.

'What in the world was that all about?' Rebecca asked when they were out of earshot.

'Crazy old thing,' Maggie said. Yet as much as she tried to pass off Mrs. Johnston's remarks, they gnawed away at her.

She didn't know why, but she suddenly felt afraid.

★　★　★

The restaurant David chose was a nice little place with red plaid wallpaper, beamed ceilings and a blazing fireplace. It was a charming room with lots of cozy atmosphere. The food was surprisingly good, the service excellent. The dinner conversation, it seemed, was devoted almost exclusively to Mrs. Johnston.

'Is she balmy or what?' Maggie wanted to know.

David chuckled. 'Yes, she's a bit odd, I must admit, but quite harmless.'

'What's this thing she has about painting everything white?' Rebecca asked.

'The house was once a nursing home. Mrs. Johnston and her husband ran it.'

'That old prune is married?' Rebecca asked, quite surprised.

'Her husband's paralyzed.'

27

'He must have been the man snoozing in the wheelchair. Remember, Maggie?'

'Yes,' David said, 'that's Mr. Johnston. He's a great old guy. Unfortunately Mrs. Johnston doesn't treat him too kindly. Nobody can figure out why she ever married him, disliking him as she obviously does.' David sighed. 'Love sometimes doesn't last long, unfortunately, which is too bad.'

'Are your rooms white also?' Rebecca asked.

'No, poor Mrs. Johnston was quite upset with me at first when I hired a couple of the local boys to come in and paint my little apartment. I didn't tell her what I was doing until it was well under way. Lucky for me she's somewhat of a tightwad. She wouldn't spend a nickel to have it repainted white so she more or less accepted it after she saw it. Naturally she raised my rent.' He laughed as he carved a piece off his steak. 'She's odd, all right, but it is the only place in town where you can get a room.'

'You should build yourself a motel,' Rebecca suggested.

'There really isn't any call for one. As I

told you, our tourist traffic is practically nil.' He put the piece of steak in his mouth and chewed.

Rebecca patted his arm. 'Well, if old Mrs. Johnston gets to be too much for you, you can always rent a couple of rooms from me and Maggie.'

He swallowed hard, giving Rebecca the strangest look. 'Yes, that would be nice,' he said. He averted his eyes and busied himself with carving another slice of meat. When he looked up he was smiling. 'Of course, the local churchgoers wouldn't look too kindly on my living in a house occupied by two beautiful and eligible women. We'd be the scandal of Pinebrook.'

Rebecca smiled. 'Good. Maybe it'll liven things up around here.'

'Rebecca,' Maggie admonished with a smile.

'Incidentally,' Rebecca said, 'Maggie and I noticed something rather peculiar during our little walk around the town this afternoon.'

'Oh? What was that?'

'Everybody here seems to have a penchant for white doors. I thought old

Mrs. Johnston was strange with her all-white house, but everyone seems to have a thing for white. Every house we saw had a white front door. What's the significance of that?'

David looked sly. He bent his head and concentrated on his steak. 'The original inhabitants of this area were the Maidu Indians. They were a very superstitious lot and the white doors you see around here are a throwback to one of their superstitions.'

'The *what* Indians?' Rebecca asked.

'Maidu. It's believed that they migrated from Russia. From Siberia, to be exact. Thousands of years ago there was no such thing as the Bering Strait, which separates North America from Asia — Alaska from Russia. It was all one solid piece of land. Tribes looking for food and warmer climates crossed over what is now the Bering Strait and kept moving south. The Maidus were one of them, historians believe. There are still a lot of them around. They settled mostly in the Feather and American river valleys. We owe our steam baths to them.'

'Our steam baths?' Rebecca laughed.

'Yes. The Maidus and their neighbors to the north, the Pomo Indians, were very adept at constructing all sorts of buildings like dance halls and meeting houses.'

'Dance halls? You're putting me on.'

'No, really. They used them for religious ceremonies and other rituals. They also built what they called sweat-houses. They were made out of reeds and bark, and inside the Indians sprinkled water over a pile of hot stones to produce steam. Every day the men took steam baths. They slept in those sweat-houses and spent much of the winter inside them.'

'Without their women? Very interesting,' Rebecca said. 'But what does all this have to do with white doors?'

'Nothing actually, except that the Maidus were very big on bleaching everything white. They said it dispelled evil spirits.'

Maggie leaned into the conversation. 'And I suppose there are evil spirits in Pinebrook?'

David gave an indifferent shrug. 'Some think there are.' He speared a piece of meat. 'As I said, the people around here are very superstitious.'

'Old Mrs. Johnston said something about evil this afternoon,' Rebecca said.

Maggie suddenly frowned at her. She wanted to forget what Mrs. Johnston had said.

'Oh?' David appeared not to be interested but, despite Maggie's frown and David's seeming indifference, Rebecca went on.

'Yes. She told Maggie that the house we're renting is evil.'

'Rebecca, please,' Maggie said sternly. 'Let's not discuss that.'

Rebecca studied her sister for a moment. 'What's with you, Mag? You look all upset.'

Maggie sighed. 'Oh, I don't know, Rebecca. I suppose I'm just tired from the trip and all. I just feel all on edge for some reason or other. I let that old woman get to me. Forgive me, Mr. McCloud. Would you mind terribly if I went back to the rooming house? I'm afraid I'm not very good company this evening.'

'But you haven't finished your dinner,' he said.

'I've had all I want,' she said, getting out of her chair. She wanted to be alone with her thoughts. Sitting next to Rebecca only served to remind her of the evil in her past. Was that same evil catching up with her again? No, she must not think of that ever again, she reminded herself.

David stood up. 'Well, if you feel you must leave, I'll drive you back, of course.'

'No, please. Don't let me spoil your evening. It isn't far. I can find my way easily enough. Good night,' she said quickly and turned and walked out of the restaurant.

'Do you think your sister will be all right?' David asked Rebecca.

Rebecca shrugged. 'She gets like that sometimes. Don't pay her any mind. She's still pretty upset about losing her husband. Rod was a terrific guy.' She sipped from her water glass. 'I'm actually quite concerned about Maggie. She hasn't been acting like herself lately.'

'How do you mean?'

'Oh, I don't know. She's prone to tempers of late. She has always been a quiet, sensible kind of girl. Now, however,

33

she's turned into a stranger. The least little thing sets her off. You saw what I mean. She's been kind of moody since she had that little talk with Mrs. Johnston.'

'What happened with Mrs. Johnston?'

'Oh, we ran in to her on the porch and she told Maggie we were making a mistake leasing Heather House . . . that the house was evil or something like that. Maggie got all upset about it. I think she would have really gotten rude if I hadn't tugged her away.'

'Did Mrs. Johnston explain what she meant by saying the house was evil?'

'No, that's just it. All Mrs. Johnston said was that we were making a mistake, that the house was evil, and *wham*, Maggie got all uptight.'

'I wonder what possessed Mrs. Johnston to say a thing like that?'

'Well, if you remember, you yourself said some people believe Heather Lambert's ghost is still roaming around in that old place.'

David chuckled. 'Oh, that. Well, everyone around here thinks Heather Lambert *is* still sitting up at that tower window waiting for her beloved husband. But you can be assured, Heather Lambert is quite dead and buried. This is a small town with small people who have small minds. They invented that ghost nonsense because they had nothing to occupy themselves with. It's like painting their doors white. It means absolutely nothing, but you could never convince the townsfolk of that. They believe a white door wards off evil and, come hell or high water, nobody will paint his door any other color but white.'

'Is your door white?'

David laughed. 'My door, dear Rebecca — if I may be so bold as to call you Rebecca — is painted a very bright red.'

Rebecca threw back her head and laughed.

'Coffee?' David asked as he motioned to the waitress.

'No. I think I should get back to the room and make sure Maggie is all right.'

'I wouldn't worry about it if I were you. You two had a very long drive. You've spent the last month or two closing down your old life and planning to start a new

35

one. Your sister is most likely finding it more difficult to adjust than you. She'll be fine once she's settled in.'

'That's what I'm afraid of,' Rebecca remarked.

'I don't understand.' The waitress appeared and David asked for the check.

'I'm afraid once Maggie gets settled in that house, nothing short of a stick of dynamite will get her out of there.'

'So what's wrong with that? It really is a very fine house; this is a very nice town. I admit it is not a very thriving place, but you have only a short drive to find a major city where you can let your hair down. All in all, I think you will find Pinebrook ideal.'

'Oh, I don't have any objections to the town or the people. It's that house that worries me.'

'Look,' David said, taking her hand, 'the house is nothing more than a house. It's big and rambling but it is in excellent condition and it will make a lovely home for both of you. And if the ghost of Heather Lambert gives you any trouble, just call and I'll come charging to the rescue on my trusty white steed.'

'I suppose I am making a mountain out of this thing, but in view of Maggie's strange behavior today I can't help but worry.'

'Come on,' David said, putting down money for the check the waitress had left. 'Let's go collect your sister and I'll drive you out through our grape fields. They're really beautiful at night and the aroma is delicious.'

'You're on,' Rebecca said.

But when they got back to Mrs. Johnston's they could not collect Maggie because Maggie was not there.

'She didn't come in,' Mrs. Johnston told them. 'I saw her walking down the street, get in her car and drive away.'

'Drive away? Where?' asked Rebecca.

Mrs. Johnston straightened her back. 'Now, I am sure I haven't the slightest idea. She said nothing to me and if she had I doubt if I would have allowed myself to listen to her. Personally, I will be happy when you and your sister are out of here tomorrow.'

Rebecca bristled. David stepped between

the two women and asked, 'Did you happen to see in which direction Mrs. Garrison headed?'

Mrs. Johnston nodded to the north. 'That way.' Toward, Rebecca thought but did not say, the Lambert house.

'She's just gone for a drive. Come on, let me show you our vineyards,' David said. He took her arm and walked down the steps, leaving Mrs. Johnston sitting in her rocker on the front porch.

Rebecca let herself be helped into David's car. After he got behind the wheel and they had started down the road, Rebecca said, 'I am worried about Maggie.'

'Maybe you two need to develop a little independence. You seem to be awfully tied to one another.'

'Oh, I don't think I'd say that.' After a moment, however, she added, 'Now that I think of it, the only time we were apart was when we went on our honeymoons.'

'Well, at least you took separate honeymoons,' David said with a laugh. 'At least that shows some independence.'

'I must admit I felt like a fish out of water the whole time Maggie and Rod were in Scotland.'

'Scotland?'

'Maggie and Rod honeymooned over there for a week. His people came from there. I thought she'd never come home.'

'That is not very healthy — you realize that, don't you?' he asked.

'Oh, I don't know. Maggie is the only family I have. We'd be lost without each other.'

'How can you speak for your sister? Maybe she doesn't feel the same way as you do.'

'Not Maggie. I know her. She'd just be lost without me.'

'How do you know? You've never tested that.'

Rebecca studied him for a minute. 'What are you trying to do, Mr. McCloud, turn me against my sister?' She was smiling. 'We love each other very much.'

'Loving a sister and living her life for her are two entirely different things. You should let Maggie go her own way and you should go yours.'

'But we do.'

'Do you? You wanted to chase after

Maggie a second or two ago. Don't you think she can look out for herself?'

Rebecca sighed. 'Maybe I don't want her to. I guess I have allowed Maggie to run things for me. I'm not exactly the most level-headed girl in the world. Maggie's always there to pick up after me. I've grown to depend on her too much, I know, but I can't help it.' She gazed out the car window. 'She really fought me tooth and nail about moving here to Pinebrook. I won out in the end, of course. Maggie always gives me my own way.'

'I for one am glad you are going to be living here. Pinebrook needs a spark of life and I am pleased it came in the form of you and your sister, Maggie.'

Rebecca laughed. 'Now how can I argue with you if you are going to say such nice things as that?'

They were driving through open fields. David eased the car to the edge of the road, switched off the lights and cut the motor. Music was playing softly on the radio. He turned in his seat and took Rebecca's hand. 'I hope we will have a lot more arguments like this,' he said, drawing her close.

'I thought you were going to show me vineyards?'

'They're in my eyes if you will look closely,' he whispered. 'You're very beautiful, you know.'

Rebecca gave a soft little whimper as his arms tightened around her. Her arms moved around his neck. She felt his body, hard and demanding, pressing against hers.

'I think I'm going to like Pinebrook,' she whispered.

3

Maggie drove blindly along the road. If anyone had asked her destination she would have said she did not know, yet way back in the deep recesses of her mind she knew perfectly well where she was going.

There was a moon, creamy bright, hanging suspended like a huge pearl in the purple-black sky. A soft, murmuring breeze blew across the empty landscape. The windows of the Mercedes were rolled down, letting the aromas of the night drift in all around her. A calm, heavy hush lay over everything — everything, that was, except Maggie's thoughts. Her mind seethed. She was afraid, but did not know the reason for her fear. She had to prove to herself that it was not the house she was afraid of, because there was nothing there to fear.

Mrs. Johnston had said the place was evil. Maggie had gotten an entirely different impression of Heather House. To her it seemed like a refuge, a safe harbor from all those other evils in her old world. The house must not prove to be a problem; she'd had enough problems for one lifetime.

Across the wide valley the smoke-gray peaks of the Diablo Range hemmed her in like the tall, thick walls of a prison. She was a long way from her cozy little apartment on that busy city boulevard. She missed the blinking sign of the all-night market down the street, the honking horns, the scurrying people.

She'd been alive there with Rod and their life together — troubled as it sometimes had been. She felt a sudden pang of sadness when she realized she would never go back there again. One could never go back; she'd learned that early in life. A second helping of anything was never as satisfying as the first.

Rebecca wasn't like that. Rebecca enjoyed gorging herself with the same old things until she succeeded in squeezing the very life out of them — men, particularly.

Rebecca.

Maggie's fears flared up again and she pressed her foot down heavily on the accelerator.

But why was she afraid of Rebecca? There was no reason for her to be afraid. Yes, Rebecca had caused trouble between her and Rod long ago, but that was in the past. Rod was dead.

She frowned and shook her head. Was Rod dead? They'd never recovered his body. Somehow it seemed impossible to think of him as being dead. Besides, Rod had been a strong swimmer.

As she rounded the curve she saw the house in the distance. It looked pink and lovely under the creamy autumn moon, its windows smiling at her, its walls opened wide, welcoming her into their embrace.

She wondered how there could be evil in so beautiful a place as Heather House. She pressed down harder on the accelerator and sped toward it, as though being pulled by a magnetic force.

As she got nearer she saw that Heather House was not entirely dark. Maggie looked at the light in the tower window. There was no electricity, she remembered David telling them; it had to be a lamp. Sophie's possibly.

She pulled the car up in front of the moon-drenched patio garden and sat there admiring the beauty of the place. It was like something out of a fairytale, all bathed in a magical light that set it apart from anything real. Nothing moved; everything was still, frozen in time. Maggie got out of the car and closed the door gently, afraid that any sound might shatter the delicate tranquility of the place.

She chose the largest of the keys given her by David McCloud. It slipped silently into the lock and turned without making a sound. The door swung open on well-oiled hinges and the house yawned before her, pulling her inside.

'Sophie,' she called softly, 'it's me, Maggie Garrison.'

No answer. The place was as quiet and lush as thick velvet.

'Sophie,' she called again, but she only heard the echo of her own voice as it floated over the dark interior. She walked on tiptoes over the bare, cold tiled foyer, not wanting to disturb the black, comforting solitude. She stepped down into the sunken living room with its lofty windows and its beamed ceiling. She fumbled for the light switch on the wall beside her. The dull little click confirmed that there was no electricity.

Maggie pulled off her light coat and dropped it, together with her gloves and purse, on a long refractory table that sat behind the imposing divan. She sank into the softness of the couch and let the room wrap itself around her.

She was here, she told herself, sitting in the dim moonlit room, and there was nothing to be afraid of. She kicked off her shoes and tucked her feet under her. It was so peaceful. At long last she could relax and think clearly. It had been so long since she had been able to relax and think about herself and her life without the interference of Rebecca.

Mrs. Johnston had been wrong. Evil could not possibly reside in Heather House. She sighed. Perhaps someday, if her hopes were to be realized, Rod would come to Heather House and find her and her life would be complete again.

Sitting in the safety and comfort of this house, she felt she could think about Rebecca and not get upset. She could not be angry or annoyed with anyone now that she was inside the house's walls. Why she had felt tense and unnerved today she did not understand, but that was all in the past. She would never feel like that again because her future seemed suddenly secure in this lovely house far away from all troubles.

Perhaps she should speak to David about buying Heather House. But Rebecca would never hear of it. Maggie shrugged. Let Rebecca wander if she chose. Rebecca always brought trouble. Rod would return, and Rebecca would settle down some-place else and never make trouble for them again. Perhaps Rebecca might fall in love with David McCloud and marry again.

Yes, Maggie thought with a sigh, everything was going to be beautiful again — in time.

She stirred. She felt something disturb

her hair. She sat forward and looked around. There was nothing; just the still, weighty presence of the room itself. She started to relax back against the cushions of the divan again, and thought she heard someone sigh.

'Sophie?' she called softly.

No one answered.

Maggie got up and went toward the row of windows that looked out onto the garden patio. Perhaps one was open, causing a draft. But the windows were all locked and secured. There was a large, ornate candelabrum perched atop a brooding concert grand piano that dominated one corner. She went to it and found a box of wax matches beside it. She lit the candles, one by one, bringing the living room to light.

In the flickering candlelight her safe feelings about the place were doubly confirmed. It was more beautiful than she'd remembered from this afternoon. The furniture gave a protective element to her surroundings. Nothing could ever hurt her in so strong and powerful a place as this.

She walked from the living room to the library, holding the candelabrum in front of her.

'Sophie?'

The library was empty, as were the other rooms beyond it. Maggie retraced her steps, going back through the living room, across the foyer and into the dining room and the rooms at its back. There was no sign of Sophie to be found anywhere. In the foyer, she looked up the wide Spanish staircase and remembered the lovely bedroom at the top. She would sleep there tonight, she decided on the spur of the moment.

She did not care whether it had not been dusted or cleaned, or whether the bed was made up or not. She did not care if Rebecca worried. She couldn't leave Heather House now that she'd come. She felt very safe here. She could not face that white, sterile room in Mrs. Johnston's house. If evil were anywhere, it was there in that stark house with its strange housekeeper. No, she wanted to stay here where she knew that Rod would someday find her.

Slowly she mounted the stairs. Her footsteps were silent on the tiles. In the upper hall she glanced down the corridor to where David had earlier said stairs led up to the tower. There was no sign of life or light. Sophie might be asleep up there with the door closed and a night light burning softly in the window. Maggie wouldn't disturb her.

The door to the master bedroom stood open. The light from her candles made the walls shimmer. To her surprise, the bed had been turned down, showing crisp, fresh sheets. There was a glass of milk sitting on the nightstand, together with two small biscuits. The milk was warm, the biscuits fresh.

Maggie ran her fingers over the top of the bureau and her fingertips came away clean. Sophie had obviously spent the afternoon dusting and polishing. In the candlelight the room looked immaculate.

She set the candelabrum on top of the bureau in front of a massive gilt mirror and studied her reflection in the glass. There was something different about her, something she couldn't quite put her finger on. She touched her hair. It had never felt so soft and silky before. And her eyes had a brighter gleam to them. Her complexion seemed smoother, creamier, flawless. She looked almost young again.

Maggie picked up the candelabrum and went back downstairs. She moved more quickly, more confidently. This was her house, she told herself. If she wanted to make a noise, who was to say she could not? She trotted down the steps, being careful to keep the candles steady. She found her purse and her shoes where she'd left them — but her gloves were missing.

'That's odd,' she said to the empty room. Perhaps Sophie picked them up with the thought in mind of washing them for her, but they were new gloves. She'd worn them for the first time this evening.

'Oh well,' she said aloud with a shrug. Maybe she'd been wrong. Perhaps she hadn't worn her gloves after all, or perhaps she'd left them on the seat of the car. It didn't really matter.

Back upstairs she again studied her

reflection in the mirror. She ran her comb through her hair. To her complete puzzlement the comb did not seem to erase the dishevelment. Her hair was as unruly as when she'd first glimpsed herself in the mirror. She combed harder, faster. The comb had no effect whatsoever. Her hair continued to look in need of a good combing.

She tossed the comb on top of the dresser. She'd attend to her hair in the morning after she'd retrieved her luggage from Mrs. Johnston's.

The sudden slamming of the door made her whirl around. The sound was so loud, so unexpected, that she let out a tight little gasp. As the echo of the bang drifted into silence, Maggie thought she heard someone laugh. It was an eerie kind of laugh, soft and far, far away. She went to the door and tried the knob. The knob refused to turn; the door would not open. She yanked hard, but the door remained firmly, definitely shut.

'It's stuck,' she said as she continued to try to pull the door open. A sudden draft from somewhere, she guessed. But the laugh? Who had laughed? Was little Sophie outside playing tricks on her? She remembered David mentioned that Sophie wasn't altogether right in the head. Perhaps she was playing tricks.

Maggie pounded on the door. 'Sophie! Sophie!'

She didn't feel particularly angry or afraid. What was there to fear from a stuck door or a silly girl who was playing pranks? She had, after all, intended to sleep in this room anyway, so what did it matter if the door was closed? Tomorrow Sophie would find the door closed and would manage to get it opened. Tomorrow she'd have a carpenter come and plane the edge if that was what was needed.

She found herself smiling. The closed door suddenly represented even more protection from the world outside. She went over to the bed and without further worry began to undress. Tomorrow would come and after it would come more tomorrows, each filled to overflowing with peace and tranquility and happiness.

'Yes, tomorrow,' Maggie said as she

slipped in between the cool, clean sheets. 'Tomorrow will be wonderful.'

She'd never felt so tired. She looked at the flickering candles. She was much too tired to get up and extinguish them. They'd burn themselves out in time . . . just as Rebecca would do.

Her eyes drooped closed.

Just before she drifted into sleep, she thought she caught the scent of heather.

★   ★   ★

Outside it was later and darker despite the fullness of the moon. A threatening, patchy overcast had moved quickly across the sky. Mrs. Johnston hid herself behind one of the tall palm trees that dotted the garden patio of Heather Lambert's old house. She watched David and Rebecca hurry out the front door and head toward his automobile, which was parked behind Maggie's Mercedes. Her own antique car was parked in a clump of trees a short way down the road. The old woman's white dress looked almost transparent in the moonlight.

She was not particularly surprised to see Rebecca's arm slip around David McCloud's waist. She'd sized up the girl the minute she laid eyes on her. That kind always threw themselves at every man they met, she told herself.

Her eyes moved upward, remembering the flickering light in the bedroom window. The other woman, older, more sensible, not quite as pretty, was the one to be most wary of. She would be the problem. The younger one could easily be dealt with; it was the older sister — Maggie Garrison — who would pose the problem.

Mrs. Johnston smiled to herself. She'd manage them both, just as she had managed the others . . .

Rebecca and David were walking quickly toward the car, almost running. It was easy to see that they had not the best intentions in mind as they hurried away from the Lambert house, Mrs. Johnston thought. It would not be the first time she'd caught David McCloud sneaking girls into his rooms. She did not approve, of course, but David was a good tenant

. . . reliable, steady and he paid well for his accommodations. There were times, Mrs. Johnston told herself, that she found it better to close her eyes to things.

Secretly she wished they'd hurry and get away. It would not go well for her if she were found here at this house, especially tonight. She glanced up at the full moon and watched a lazy cloud pass across its face. If it had to be done, tonight was the night she should finish it. But she knew that at least the ground-work had been laid and tomorrow it would be over with.

The cloud covered the moon, then drifted away, leaving it to shine ominously down over everything. This was the night the souls carried their lanterns over the earth, seeking a place of rest. It was Samhain, summer's end, the hallowed evening for roaming spirits, shimmering ghosts, black cats . . . The night fairies, witches and elves alike came out to do their evil.

Rebecca glanced back at the house just before getting into the car. There was a strange, frightening look about her. She hesitated. David said something which Mrs. Johnston did not hear. Rebecca slipped quickly into the seat and in an instant the car roared to life and shot down the driveway and out onto the road.

Mrs. Johnston breathed a sigh of relief and pushed herself out from behind the protection of the palm tree. She found her hands trembling, her body tense with anticipation. She walked quickly across the garden patio.

More than once she glanced up at the bedroom window on the second floor. It was dark now. The flickering candles were gone from the window. The only light was that in the tower.

★   ★   ★

Maggie lay curled up on her pillow. Her head was filled with the most wonderful dreams: dreams of Rod and the bright flowered patio, and the handsome house with its thick pink walls and solid roof that held her and Rod safe and secure inside. She pictured herself cradled in his arms before a roaring fire, listening to the

57

soft music of a Chopin nocturne . . . their nocturne. The music's dreamy sentimentality drifted over them, bringing with it a languid melancholy that fused them into one being, one soul. She could hear Rod's voice as he murmured Shelley's lovely words, the music fitting perfectly the meter of the poem:

When I arose and saw the dawn,
I sighed for thee;
When light rode high, and the dew
  was gone,
And moon lay heavy on flower and tree,
And the weary day turned to her rest,
Lingering like an unloved guest,
I sighed for thee.

Maggie sighed for want of him and turned comfortably in her sleep. As she turned the deep blue contentment of her dream began to fade. She tried to hold on to it, but bit by bit the dark lushness of her peacefulness was being torn away. Fragments of light colors filtered onto the backs of her eyes, lighting the dream, sending it out into the bright blaze of a scorching sun. The nocturne gradually dwindled to a whisper and then it was gone completely. The ease with which she breathed suddenly became labored. A choking in her throat brought on a spasm of coughing. Icy fingers were tightening around her throat, cutting off her wind.

Panic opened her eyes. There was a brilliant glare in the room. Smoke hung around her so impenetrable she could barely see. Her eyes watered from the billows of smoke. She bolted up in the bed and heard the crackling and saw the reddish-orange fingers of hot, scorching fire eating their way up the draperies.

Maggie screamed and leaped out of bed. The fire was confined to the tall barred window nearest her bed. She screamed again, seeing the flames eat faster, more hungrily, at the window's trappings. She raced madly toward the door. She yanked at the knob, yelling at the top of her lungs. The door was stuck solid. It refused to budge. A spasm of coughing made her double over and almost knocked her to her knees.

'Help! Help me!' she yelled, but her

screams ended in choking coughs. She tried to think of what she should do. The fire would engulf her if she did not do something . . . anything.

Staggering across the room, heedless of the heat and the fire, she grabbed hold of the flaming draperies and yanked with all her might. The heavy brocade plunged down, almost enveloping her. First one, then the other panel was yanked from the rod. The hooks that held them were old and rusted with age; they came unhooked from their support without much effort.

Maggie felt the fire in her hands but she had no time to worry about possible burns. The pile of blazing drapes lay in a heap like a bonfire. She saw the fire begin to eat its way into the carpeting. She swept the heavy coverlet together with its blanket from the bed and threw it over the flames. She cast herself down on top of them and rolled back and forth, beating, pounding the flames into submission, smothering the fire until nothing remained but whispers of smoke that seeped out from under the edges of the coverlet.

A large, empty vase sat on a console. She seized it and ran into the adjoining bathroom, filling the vase with water. Back in the bedroom she poured the contents down onto the smoldering heap, again and again, until it was nothing more than an unrecognizable sodden pile of rags.

With the vase dangling from her hand, she staggered toward the window and tried to raise the sash. Like the door, it would not budge. In desperation she lifted her arm and sent the vase crashing through the glass panes, shattering the moldings that held them in their intricate pattern. A rush of cool, clean air flew in at her. She sucked it deep into her lungs, resting her head against the frame, not caring about the jagged shards of jutting glass so near her face.

She sagged motionless at the window, breathing deeply, feeling the thick ache in her head, the stinging in her eyes. Her heart was pounding in her breast; every nerve of her body was screaming out at her. The smell of burned cloth hung about her.

When she stepped away from the window, her foot bumped something heavy and solid. She glanced down. The candelabrum lay on its side, its candles charred and almost completely melted. Maggie frowned down at it. She had not put the candelabrum there; she'd left it on the bureau, completely on the other side of the room.

Her skin still felt scorched. She went into the bathroom and time and again splashed water up over her face and eyes, relishing the cold, clean relief it brought. After what seemed forever, her throat felt less constricted. She let herself slip to the cool, hard-tiled floor, where she lay with her head cradled on her arm.

Suddenly she started to cry. From deep within came uncontrolled tears and sobs and she gave herself up to her fear, crying softly until her exhaustion weighed down her body. She lay, thinking about the burning draperies and the candelabrum that had somehow found its way under the bedroom window. How it had gotten there she did not know, but she knew one thing for sure — she had not put it there herself and it could not have gotten there all by itself. Someone had obviously sneaked into the room and moved the lighted candles to where they could ignite the drapes, setting fire to the room.

But who? And more importantly, *why*? How had whoever it was gotten into the room? The door was stuck. A disturbing little chill ran down her spine. Had the door been locked or bolted from the outside?

She rolled over onto her back, watching the smoke cling to the ceiling. Gradually it was growing thinner, drifting outside where its poison would be purified by the night air. Suddenly a new fear made her sit up. If someone had tried to burn her alive, whoever it was might still be lurking in the house, waiting to make sure of the results of the heinous act. With the fire out, might they try something else?

She hurried across the bedroom to the door and again twisted the knob. To her complete surprise the door opened. It swung back, releasing the remaining smoke from the room. Maggie ran out and down the tiled staircase. She flew on bare feet until she reached the front door and ran out into the night. A cold, chilling wind nipped at her.

She realized belatedly that she was wearing nothing but her slip. Hurrying to her car, she slipped behind the wheel and slammed the door and locked herself in. She sat there, panting until her breathing became normal, thankful for the cleanness of the air and the safety of the well-constructed vehicle.

She'd no sooner decided to go back to Mrs. Johnston's when she remembered that the car keys were in her handbag, upstairs in the bedroom. She slumped down in the seat and tried to think. Mrs. Johnston had said the house was evil, but something human had set the candles by the drapes. Someone had tried to kill her.

The thought was so unnatural, so foreign to her that she had difficulty accepting it. She was just a harmless, almost middle-aged woman who had no enemies. What threat could she represent to anyone? Besides, to the best of her knowledge, no one knew she had come to the house and was sleeping in that room.

Sophie.

The name popped into her head. David McCloud had said Sophie was considered a bit eccentric. But surely that harmless little woman would have no reason to injure her. Sophie barely knew her. And, from what Maggie had seen of Sophie, she was sure that she was not capable of doing such a horrible thing as burning someone alive.

Or was she?

David McCloud would surely not lease a house that came equipped with a homicidal maniac. Yet Sophie was the only possible person to know she was asleep in that room; she lived here full-time. Certainly she had heard Maggie drive up and had heard her calling, even though she had chosen not to answer. What if she wasn't asleep in the tower room as Maggie had supposed? Had she heard and seen Maggie and looked upon her as an enemy, a usurper who threatened to take the house away — so she had crept down from the tower and locked the bedroom door after moving the candelabrum under the window?

Ridiculous. That poor soul wouldn't have any reason to do her harm. It was inconceivable that Sophie would want to kill her. And if she did, she certainly would not want to burn down the house in the process. No, it couldn't have been poor little Sophie. She would not destroy the roof over her own head.

But if not Sophie, then who?

Her head started to spin. She rested it back against the seat and tried to block from her mind the hundreds of questions that seemed to be spinning around inside her.

After a moment she sighed and straightened up. She glanced at the clock on the dashboard. It was almost one o'clock. She'd thought it was much later. As she noted the time she caught a glimpse of movement. Something flickered a short distance in front of the car. She reached down and flipped on the headlights, thankful that she had no need of the ignition key for the lights to work.

Maggie's hand flew to her mouth, stifling a scream. There, plainly visible in front of the Mercedes was a small, gnarled figure dressed completely in black. The face was sharp and ugly. When the lights hit the figure it threw back its hands in horror. Then the figure relaxed again. If there was such a thing on earth as a witch, Maggie was convinced she was looking at it.

The old hag stood for a moment as though hypnotized by the light. Then she threw back her head, showing a toothless grin and laughed up at the sky.

Maggie cowered in the seat, trying to find refuge behind the steering wheel. The figure was coming toward her. The closer it got the more frightening it became. The eyes were like red burning coals. The lips were pulled back, showing the black hole of the mouth. There was a grotesque wart on her chin and long, gray straggling hair cascading down from an outlandish black hat with narrow brim and tall peak.

The face pressed itself against the window. Maggie was afraid to look at it. A thin, bony finger with black, tapered nail tapped on the glass. The mouth moved; the eyes blazed in at her.

Maggie forced herself to look, to convince herself she wasn't caught up in some terrible nightmare. Her look became a stare. There was something familiar about the shape of the face despite the red, glowing eyes and the ugly wart.

'Sophie!' she exclaimed, breathing a sigh of relief. Quickly she rolled down the window.

'I hope I didn't scare you too much,' Sophie said in her little girl's voice. 'The church had a Halloween party. I scared all the children.' She laughed a cackling kind of laugh and did a little dance with her broom. 'I really scared the lot of them.'

'Sophie,' Maggie sighed and breathed again, 'you really did frighten the dickens out of me.'

'Good. Good,' Sophie said, again dancing in a circle with her broom. 'I scared you, I scared you,' she sang in her childish voice. The little sing-song dance broke off abruptly. Sophie's face threw off its grin. She came close to the window again. 'What are you doing out here? You said you'd be back tomorrow to take care of everything.' She glanced at the way Maggie was dressed.

'Why are you dressed like that? Were you going to a party, too?'

Maggie thought about the fire, the thick, choking smoke, the locked door, the shattered window. 'Have you been at the party all evening, Sophie?' she asked.

'Yes. Why? Miss Heather said I could go.' She stuck out her lower lip far enough for a bird to perch on it. 'You said you'd be here tomorrow. I did my work. I cleaned as much as I could.'

'No, it's all right, Sophie. I don't mind your going to the party. I just wondered if you'd been in town all evening.'

Sophie tossed back her head. 'Now that would be telling, wouldn't it? I can have secrets if I want to.' She cackled suddenly and again hopped around with her broom. She was gone before Maggie had a chance to call after her.

4

Maggie clicked off the headlights and sat there in the dark trying to think, but none of her thoughts had direction. One thing was obvious, however. Whether she stayed in the house tonight or went back to Mrs. Johnston's, she would have to go back inside; she couldn't stay out here in the car dressed as she was.

Never one to put off what had to be done, she pushed open the car door and got out. She went quickly across the patio, seeing the splinters of glass that had fallen from the second-story window. There was a distinct smell of burned cloth as she passed under the portico and went inside.

The moment she closed the door she heard scurrying footsteps. Sophie appeared at the top of the stairs with a candle in her hand. The sight of the flickering flame brought a tinge of fear back into Maggie's mind.

'Miss Heather did something bad.'

Maggie looked up. Sophie had discarded her peaked hat. The wart was gone from her chin and the black removed from her teeth.

'There's been a small fire,' Maggie said as she started up the stairs. Halfway up, she hesitated. What was she doing? It was quite possible that Sophie had started the fire. She stood where she was, afraid to advance any farther just in case she was walking into some kind of trap.

'She was bad again. She broke a window and burned things up.'

'No,' Maggie said softly, tightening her hand on the railing. 'I was asleep in that room, Sophie. The drapes caught on fire. I had to pull them down in order to extinguish the flames. I broke the window.'

It was as if she hadn't spoken. 'Miss Heather is always doing bad things like that. She wanted to go to the party but she couldn't so she did a bad thing.' The girl's eyes suddenly opened wide and she stared down at Maggie with sudden terror in her face. 'She makes me do bad things sometimes. She's always making me do bad things.'

'What are you saying?' Maggie gasped. 'Did you set the fire, Sophie?' She found herself trembling.

'No,' Sophie gasped. 'Oh, no. I don't think I did. But sometimes . . . '

'Sophie,' Maggie snapped, 'did you move the candles under the window? Did you cause the drapes to catch on fire? Answer me.'

Sophie looked wildly around, as though searching for somewhere to run, somewhere to hide. 'Miss Heather . . . she sometimes makes me . . . I didn't do anything wrong. I didn't do anything.' She was beginning to babble. Her lips quivered and unintelligible sounds came out of her mouth. Maggie watched as Sophie's frail little body started to shake all over, her eyes darting back and forth like those of a terrified animal.

Forgetting her own qualms, Maggie rushed up the steps. She grabbed Sophie by the shoulders.

'I didn't!' Sophie wailed. 'I don't think . . . '

'Sophie,' Maggie said sharply, shaking the girl, 'control yourself.'

Sophie sobbed and tried to struggle free of Maggie's grip but Maggie held her firmly. She pulled Sophie against her and hugged her tightly until she felt Sophie begin to calm down.

'It's all right, Sophie. Don't cry. It's all right. No harm's been done.'

But it wasn't all right . . . and harm *had* been done. She'd come within inches of being burned alive and here she stood holding a girl who might easily be responsible for her murder and telling her it was all right.

It seemed like she had spent her life forgiving others, saying everything was all right when it wasn't. Just like the time Rebecca had pushed her out of the tree house during a jealous rage. No real harm had been done to Maggie and when Rebecca had become almost hysterical with remorse, Maggie had hugged her — as she was now hugging Sophie — and had told her it was all right.

Poor Sophie was beside herself. Whether or not the girl had been responsible for what had happened wasn't important at the moment. Sophie continued to moan and sob against her breast. Maggie hushed her, as a mother quiets a frightened child . . . as Maggie had consoled Rebecca after some terrible prank.

'Come, Sophie. Let's make us a pot of coffee,' Maggie said softly as she felt the girl calming down a bit. 'Let's not talk about it. It's all right.'

Empathy had always been a part of Maggie's nature. As she and Sophie walked slowly downstairs Maggie remembered another night, long, long ago when she'd returned home unexpectedly to find Rebecca and Rod locked in each other's arms.

What good would it have done to make a scene, the result of which might well have meant the loss of both her sister and her husband? Whose fault it had been was immaterial. She suspected that it had been Rebecca's doing, but it did not matter. She loved Rod; she loved Rebecca. She said nothing to them; she merely closed her eyes to what she had seen and forgave them.

Of course for a while the shame and guilt they suffered after receiving Maggie's absolution was most worthwhile. She felt she'd been repaid a thousand times over for that simple act of forgiveness. But as the weeks passed she knew Rebecca and Rod had renewed their improper relationship. She could tell by looking at them that they'd been together; guilt showed easily on their faces, especially Rod's. He was weak, that she'd always known; but she loved him and he, in his way, loved her, so she closed her eyes to what was going on.

The same would be true in Sophie's case. If the girl had been responsible for the fire, Maggie would be alert to future dangers, but she doubted if the girl would prove overly dangerous in the future.

Sophie looked weird sitting at the enamel-topped kitchen table, still wearing part of her ridiculous witch's costume and makeup. She had traced dark circles under her eyes and black lines down and across her face. She resembled a storybook character who'd jumped from the page of the book and came to life.

Maggie fussed with the coffee. Sophie sat dazed and quiet, hands folded in front of her.

'Was the party fun?' Maggie asked in an effort to get the girl's mind onto more pleasing thoughts.

Sophie looked up. 'Miss Heather told me I could go. The children always expect old Sophie every year.' She made a face. 'The others don't want me there but I go anyway. The children like me.'

'I'm sure everyone likes you, Sophie.'

'No they don't. Nobody likes Sophie. They say terrible things about me when they don't think I'm listening. But I hear them. They're always talking, saying bad things about me and Miss Heather.'

'Tell me about Miss Heather,' Maggie said, trying to sound matter-of-fact. She adjusted the gas flame under the coffee-pot and came to sit down beside Sophie at the table. The single candle burning in its holder threw their faces out of proportion. Maggie decided her best tactic would be to humor the girl. 'Have you worked for her very long, Sophie?'

'Oh, yes. I was just a wee thing when I

came to live here with Miss Heather. She found me in the field. She took me home and gave me nice things to wear.'

'And where is Miss Heather now?'

'Now?' Sophie gave her a blank look. 'Upstairs, of course. She's in her room in the tower.'

'Doesn't she ever come down from the tower?' Maggie felt a tight stab of fear when she remembered the light in the tower window. Heather Lambert couldn't possibly be up there. She was dead. Everyone said so.

'Sure she does. Lots of times.'

'Why does she stay in the tower?'

'That's where she lives.'

'Will you take me to meet her?'

Sophie shook her head. 'She doesn't like to meet people.'

Maggie forced a smile and reached over to pat Sophie's hand. 'But as long as I'm her houseguest, don't you think it would be nice if I went and introduced myself to her? I really would like to meet Miss Heather.'

'No,' Sophie said sharply, pulling her hand away. 'You mustn't do that.'

'Why not?'

'Miss Heather wouldn't like it. She'd get mad. She'd do terrible things.'

Maggie thought about the fire and suddenly wondered if the possibility might exist that Miss Heather really wasn't dead, as everyone thought. Or perhaps someone else was living in this old abandoned house. Heather Lambert had once found this half-demented child in a field and had taken her in. Had Sophie emulated her by bringing home another lonely soul? A relative, perhaps?

She told herself she'd have to investigate that tower room at the earliest opportunity. She'd have to search the house from top to bottom to make sure no one other than herself, Sophie and Rebecca were living here.

Maggie got up and started to look in the cupboards for cups and saucers. There was a mirror hanging on one wall and when she passed in front of it she caught her dim reflection. The room behind her was almost in total darkness, except for the candle on the table, but she saw something in her reflection that caused her to stop and gaze at it. She stared at herself. The image was so different she almost didn't recognize it as her own. The hair was disheveled, her face drawn and peaked. There was a strange mistiness in the eyes. The face was hers, yet there was something different.

She shook herself. Remembering the terrifying experience she'd been put through, it was no wonder she looked strange. She suddenly felt foolish standing there in the dark of the kitchen wearing only a slip. No wonder she looked a fright. She touched the thinness of her slip and thought it odd that she did not feel cold . . . in fact she felt quite warm and comfortable in the snug kitchen.

It was a nice kitchen, big and roomy with lots of cabinets and work space. She'd bring in plants and start an indoor herb garden. It would be fun to cook and bake in such a delightful place.

The house was working its magic again. She almost completely dismissed the fire upstairs . . . the attempt on her life. Of course she would not be able to sleep in that lovely room tonight, she told herself.

The room would have to be well aired tomorrow. But there were other rooms, other beds. She could never go back to Mrs. Johnston's. She was here and she'd stay here . . . forever.

'Sophie?' she said, turning from her reverie. She glanced at the empty table. Sophie was gone. The kitchen was empty. The candle looked lonely burning in the center of the big table.

'Oh, well,' Maggie said as she put one cup and saucer back into the cupboard. She poured herself a cup of coffee and sat down to keep the candle company. She stared at its tiny flame, letting the dark quiet of the room nestle around her shoulders. She propped her elbows on the table and brought the cup to her lips. She cautiously tested the coffee's strength and temperature. She frowned down at the cup, crinkling her nose as an unusual aroma greeted her nostrils. It didn't smell at all like coffee should smell. The scent was familiar but it was definitely not coffee.

She put the cup down and stared at it for a moment, trying to identify the smell.

She sniffed the air. The room seemed suddenly filled with the heavy, sweet odor . . . a most pleasing and delightful odor. It was an odor she'd smelled somewhere before. The fragrance was very familiar. She tried to think. She knew the smell, but from where?

She straightened in her chair when she remembered. 'Of course,' she said aloud to the quiet of the room. 'It's heather.' In a flash the one short week in the Scottish Highlands came tumbling back. That all-too-brief, wonderful week of love and sex and Rod.

Their honeymoon, which Rod had insisted they splurge on. One week was all they could afford, but it was a week crammed full of the most deliciously romantic memories. The quaint villages and rolling farmlands; the broad, rolling straths, Glen Moor, the Grampian Mountains. Yes, it had been a sublime week, one she would cherish forever. She recalled the tiny inn at which they'd stayed — surrounded by fields of heather. And they'd had their own private castle perfectly framed in their latticed windows.

Maggie sighed, breathing in the smell of heather.

Her sigh turned to a deep frown. Where was the fragrance coming from? The kitchen was permeated with it, and it seemed to grow more and more intense as the minutes passed.

She pushed herself away from the table and walked to the row of windows that overlooked a stretch of empty fields at the rear of the house. The moon was still there, guarding the silent, empty land. Nothing moved; nothing made a sound.

The smell of heather was becoming as thick as the smoke that had tried to suffocate her earlier. She tugged at the window and raised it. The night air drifted in, carrying with it a still-heavier wave of the smell of heather. And with the wave of heather came a figure, far in the distance. A man was walking across the field, coming directly toward her.

Maggie pressed her face against the glass and peered out into the night. The figure was familiar. Her heart started to beat faster as she recognized the long-familiar strides, the graceful swing of the arms. He was too far away to make out his face but she knew the figure well.

'Rod!' she yelled, pushing herself away from the window and rushing toward the door. She pulled it open, not caring how she was dressed or how she looked, and practically threw herself outside.

'Rod,' she called, waving her hands wildly as she ran as fast as she could toward the advancing figure. She ran into the field with tears of joy blurring her vision. She ran blindly forward. He was back. Rod was back. She knew he'd come. She knew he wasn't dead. Rod was here. Everything was perfect.

The scent of heather grew still thicker.

She almost stumbled over a tangle of weeds. She brushed the tears from her eyes. Suddenly she stopped dead.

'Rod,' she said, a little more softly as she looked to where she'd seen him. She frowned at the flat, empty land. She rubbed her eyes with the backs of her hands and smoothed back her hair.

'Rod?'

She stood there, baffled by the emptiness of the place.

She was alone. There was no one walking toward her. There was no one there in the field except herself.

'Rod!' She felt a cold tightness inside her.

She looked around. She was completely alone. There was no one there, no one but herself and the fading scent of heather.

When she returned to the house, Maggie picked up the candle from the kitchen table and went toward the living room. She could not understand what she'd seen, or what she'd thought she'd seen. Her eyes had obviously played tricks on her.

The scent of heather was gone. It might well have come about as a result of the smoke and the burnt cloth. Something had burned, producing the fragrance similar to heather; it was as simple as that. And her imagination, her longing, had conjured up a vision of Rod because she wanted him so desperately to be with her. She needed him so very much.

She felt very tired as she curled up on the couch and pulled an afghan over her. The smell of smoke lingered in the air but she did not feel threatened by it. The house would protect her, alert her to danger just as it had done earlier. Nothing would harm her, she felt sure. Whoever had set the blaze would never succeed at killing her. The house would see to that.

She'd be safe until Rod arrived. And he would come. He would find her, she said to herself as her eyes dropped closed and she snuggled deeper into the softness of the couch. She reminded herself that Sophie was wandering about somewhere in the depths of the house.

The thought did not trouble her. Poor Sophie would do her no harm. She tucked the afghan up under her chin and forced every thought out of her head. Sleep came quickly in a great untroubled quantity.

And morning came before she was ready for it. But the sounds and the smells that accompanied it tempted her out of her sleep. She stretched, luxuriating in the exquisite warmth of the room. Somewhere outside birds were chirping merrily to anyone who wanted to listen.

She heard the clatter of dishes and glanced toward the door to see Sophie carrying a breakfast tray.

'Good morning,' Maggie said brightly as she uncurled herself from the couch. Sophie merely gave her a pleasant little nod and set the tray down on the huge coffee table. 'The coffee smells delicious,' Maggie commented. Sophie didn't answer. She turned and hurried away.

Maggie smiled after her, wondering if she felt guilty about what had transpired last night.

But she wouldn't think about last night. That was in the past. Today was the beginning of a new life. Whatever came before was not to be thought of now, she told herself as she picked up the coffee cup and walked toward the window. She pushed open the casement and stood there sipping her coffee and watching the happy birds flutter and hop from branch to branch.

She finished her coffee while standing and admiring the beauty of the patio garden, the brightness of the day, the sparkle of everything around her. How good it was to be alive in so wonderful a place as this, she thought. She felt she could stand here forever.

No, she told herself, pushing herself away from the casement. There was too much that needed to be done. The bedrooms upstairs would have to be aired and cleaned. There were her trunks to send for. The electricity had to be arranged for. There was cleaning and painting and dusting and exploring.

She reminded herself of the tower room and the possibility of Sophie having moved someone else into the house. She'd search everywhere just to be sure there was no one living in the house who did not belong there.

That could wait till a little later, however. First things first. Collect Rebecca. Move in. Get settled.

She replaced her cup on the tray and buttered a cinnamon roll fresh from the oven. Nibbling on it, she trotted upstairs and into the large bedroom. The smashed window would have to be replaced immediately. The debris from the fire would have to be removed. Oh, yes, there was so much to do and she was so very anxious to get started with it all.

Her clothes smelled of smoke and after showering she felt reluctant to put them on, but she had no other alternative, she told herself. She dressed hurriedly, all the time making mental notes of things that needed to be attended to once she reached Pinebrook.

She spent a short time with Sophie, who was quiet and subdued this morning. She thought it best not to bring up last night, at least for the moment. Then she got into the Mercedes and headed for Pinebrook and Rebecca.

★   ★   ★

Mrs. Johnston gasped and dropped the feather duster she had in her hand when she saw Maggie drive up to the house, staring at Maggie as though she were seeing a ghost. She straightened herself, forcing herself to regain the composure she so suddenly lost, and leveled her eyes at Maggie, ignoring her friendly smile. 'If you're looking for your sister, you won't find her in the room,' Mrs. Johnston said with an ugly sneer on her face.

Maggie couldn't be angry or annoyed at anyone this morning. This was the very first day of her new life and nothing was going to spoil it for her. She didn't know why Mrs. Johnston had looked so surprised to see her, but then she remembered that she hadn't slept here and the old woman obviously thought she was still sound asleep upstairs in that white, sterile room.

'What are you talking about?' Maggie asked pleasantly.

'Your sister. She isn't where she should be.'

Maggie arched an eyebrow. 'Oh? And what, may I ask, is that supposed to mean?'

'Just what I said. Your sister isn't where you expect to find her.'

'Where is she?' Maggie fought to retain her good humor.

Mrs. Johnston's eyes narrowed. 'Where else? With him, of course. Mr. McCloud.' She said the name with such distaste and with such insinuation that Maggie found herself blushing slightly.

'I see,' Maggie said flatly. She actually wasn't all that surprised, knowing Rebecca. It wasn't the first time Rebecca had slept in a bed other than her own. Maggie never approved, of course, but there was little she could do about it. Rebecca had a mind of her own where men were concerned and, despite the many lectures, Rebecca remained true to her nature in that regard. Maggie certainly was no prude. She believed in physical love but not in promiscuity. Rebecca, unfortunately, didn't believe in anything.

'Are they upstairs now?' Maggie asked, trying not to look surprised or shocked. She refused to give this woman the pleasure of knowing she did not approve.

'They haven't come down,' Mrs. Johnston said, looking very righteous. 'I don't tolerate such things in my house. I want you and your sister out of here today.'

Maggie was going to ask her if she would be ordering David out as well. After all, it was his living quarters and Maggie was sure it wasn't the first time David had entertained a woman all night.

But she remembered David saying he paid very well for his rooms; Mrs. Johnston was obviously the type who looked the other way when revenue was involved.

'We have no intention of remaining in your house, Mrs. Johnston,' Maggie said. She couldn't suppress the desire to hurt. 'The room you assigned to us was most unsatisfactory . . . so much so that I found it impossible to sleep there. I'm certain my sister felt the same.'

'Regardless,' Mrs. Johnston sneered, 'you'll pay for the lodgings.'

'Gladly.' Maggie fumbled in her purse and handed the money to Mrs. Johnston, who tucked it into the pocket of her white apron. 'I'll get my sister now if you'll excuse me.' Maggie waited until the woman stepped aside. She marched past and went up the white stairway with its chipped white enamel paint.

Just as she reached the upper hall Maggie heard the sound of a door opening. At the far end of the corridor she saw Rebecca slip out of David's apartment, hugging her suit jacket in front of her. Her hair was uncombed, her clothing rumpled.

'Good morning,' Maggie said, purposely sarcastic.

Rebecca spun around and her eyes grew big as saucers. 'Maggie? What . . . ? Where did you come from?' She stood there, staring as if she'd never seen her sister before this morning.

'What do you mean, where did I come from?'

Rebecca wilted. She lowered her head and hurried into the room where she was supposed to have slept.

'You needn't look so guilty, Rebecca. This kind of behavior is hardly something new for you.'

Rebecca shrugged, gathering her pride back around her. 'I couldn't face this room,' she said. 'You couldn't either, I see,' she added, nodding to the unslept-in beds.

'No,' Maggie said coolly. 'I slept at the new house.'

'Yes, I know.'

'You know?' Maggie said, surprised.

'Yes. David and I drove out there and

92

saw the car. We went in and found you sound asleep upstairs. We didn't want to disturb you.'

'You were in that upstairs bedroom last night?' Maggie's mind started to click away. Surely Rebecca hadn't put the candelabrum under the window. Yet that old, troublesome memory nagged at her.

No, that was all in the past. Rebecca had changed. She shook off the thought. Rebecca had no reason now to set fire to that room. She had no reason to want Maggie dead. Still, when she looked directly at her sister, she saw the old familiar guilt in them.

Guilt because Maggie had found her slipping out of David McCloud's little apartment, or from something more?

But why would Rebecca want her dead? She disliked the new house, perhaps, but surely that was hardly a reason to set fire to it . . . and to her own sister as well.

Rebecca started to strip herself out of her clothes. 'I don't know what possessed you to stay in that house without any electricity, Maggie. And what in the name of heaven was all that display of nerves about in the restaurant last night? You acted very peculiarly.'

Maggie knew she was purposely putting the shoe on the other foot, trying to put the responsibility for what had happened on Maggie's reliable shoulders.

It worked.

'I don't know what got into me yesterday,' Maggie apologized. 'I suppose it was a combination of things . . . the long trip, leaving everyone behind, the excitement of the house.'

It was as if Rebecca hadn't heard or wasn't listening. 'I'm going to take a shower. Be with you in a minute.' She disappeared into the white tiled bathroom.

Maggie sat down on the side of the bed and started to undo her clothing. She could still smell the odor of smoke that clung to her black dress. She wished she'd never left the house. She could have sent Sophie into town to fetch her bags, to attend to whatever else needed to be done. The morning there had been bright and brilliant and glorious; the morning here was far from any of that.

She stripped out of her clothes and selected a fresh, clean black dress from her suitcase. She refused to let any of it affect her. She'd make the house liveable; then it would be her refuge where she would stay and wait for Rod.

★ ★ ★

Rebecca came out of the bathroom wrapped in a towel and, discarding it, began to slip into her underthings. Maggie couldn't help but see the marks on her skin, the evidence of her night with David. A tiny prick of resentment gnawed at her. At first sight David McCloud had looked very much like Rod. The thought disturbed her.

'I paid Mrs. Johnston,' Maggie commented, for want of something to take her mind off her thoughts. 'I have a shopping list and I'll have to find the electric company so they can be told to turn on the power. Then there are our trunks to be sent for.' Maggie watched Rebecca move slowly about the room. 'Do you want to come with me, or shall I pick you up later?'

'I'll come with you, of course,' Rebecca said. She gave Maggie a look of pure innocence as though surprised at the question.

'Well, hurry up then. There's a lot to be done. I smashed one of the upstairs windows last night,' she said, keeping a steady eye on Rebecca to see what her reaction would be.

There was no reaction. 'Smashed a window, did you say? How did you manage to do that?'

'There was a fire in my room.'

'A fire?' Rebecca turned and glanced at her but her eyes moved away immediately.

'Someone set fire to my room.'

Rebecca looked at her. This time her eyes didn't slip away. 'Set fire to the room? You mean that room you slept in last night?'

Maggie nodded gravely.

'You say *someone* set fire to it . . . like on purpose?'

'That's precisely what I mean.'

To Maggie's surprise Rebecca grinned.

96

'Surely you don't mean that? Surely it was an accident of some kind.'

'It was no accident. I put the candelabrum on the bureau. Someone moved it to the floor directly beneath the draperies beside the bed where I was asleep.'

'But who? Why?' Rebecca turned away and studied herself in the mirror. 'Really, Maggie, are you sure you didn't put the candles down on the night table and knock it over in your sleep? I find it hard to believe that anyone would try to burn you up. I can understand why they might want to burn that old barn to the ground, but certainly not with you inside it.' She started to brush her hair and dust herself with powder.

On the tip of Maggie's tongue was the question, 'You didn't set fire to the drapes, did you, Rebecca?' But she just could not bring herself to ask. This was her little sister. Even after what had happened so long ago she could not bring herself to suspect Rebecca of so horrible an act.

'Perhaps you're right. Maybe I did move the candelabrum next to the bed without realizing it.'

Rebecca applied her lipstick with great care, making ugly little faces at herself as she did so. 'I have a feeling about that old place,' she said. She glanced at Maggie through the mirror. 'I know, I know. I won't go into it, Maggie, but maybe old Mrs. Johnston was right. Your first night there and there's a fire that almost killed you. Maybe that's some kind of evil omen.'

'It isn't the house I have to be afraid of,' Maggie said apprehensively.

'What then?

'The house didn't set fire to itself; something living caused that fire.'

'Oh, Maggie, you are being silly. It must have been an accident on your part.'

Rebecca gave her reflection an approving nod. Maggie was puzzled by how unconcerned Rebecca seemed. 'Come on, Maggie. Let's go take care of whatever has to be taken care of. I think I'll even be glad to get moved into this house of ours just so I won't have to sleep in this room again.' She picked up her suitcases and started for the door.

Maggie felt like reminding her that she hadn't slept in this room. But she let the thought pass.

David McCloud was in the hall. When he saw them he stopped dead. 'Maggie. Good morning.' Maggie saw the quick guarded look that passed between him and Rebecca. For a second or two Maggie thought he also looked very surprised, if not shocked, to see her standing there with Rebecca.

Or had she imagined it?

5

There was something about David McCloud's expression that made Maggie suspicious. Or was it jealousy she felt? Or was it fear? She sometimes got emotions mixed up — like the time she'd found Rod and Rebecca in each other's arms. Had she been jealous because Rod was interested in Rebecca, or had she been afraid she might lose both of them? Was she now feeling envious of Rebecca for having allowed herself to be seduced by this handsome man . . . this man who reminded her so much of Rod? Ridiculous, she told herself.

'Rebecca and I have a lot to accomplish this morning, David. You'll excuse us if we hurry on.'

'But I thought I might accompany you and be of whatever service I can.' He reached out and took Rebecca's suitcases from her. When he reached for Maggie's she drew them away.

'We can manage quite well by ourselves.' She thought that sounded a bit severe so she appended, 'We've taken up enough of your valuable time as it is, David.'

'I had intended showing you about the house.'

'Oh, I doubt if that will be necessary. Sophie can show me what needs to be shown.' She saw Rebecca and David exchange furtive looks. Maggie knew her sister well enough to know that Rebecca was trying to tell him that Maggie knew all about last night. Why was he so dense as not to be able to grasp the meaning behind Rebecca's glances?

Men! David McCloud was nothing at all like her Rod. How could she ever have thought they resembled one another?

'Please. I insist,' David said. 'At least let me help you with your luggage. My day is free. I purposely arranged it so that I might be of help to you two.'

She wanted to be rid of him. The best way, she decided, was to send him on errands that would remove him from her presence. Maggie smiled, looking as charming as possible. 'You're very sweet, David.' She swung her suitcases within reach. 'You may put these in the car. And then if you would be so kind, we would appreciate your seeing about having the electricity turned on in the house. Also, I noticed a broken window in the upstairs bedroom. We'll need a carpenter. I'm afraid the frame is smashed as well as the panes.'

David frowned. 'But there isn't a broken window in the place. I've been very careful not to let anything like that go unrepaired.'

'I broke it,' Maggie said flatly. She did not elaborate. She knew as soon as he and Rebecca were alone she'd tell him everything . . . if he didn't know already. She saw that he was going to question her so she said quickly, 'Accidents will happen. Naturally, I will pay whatever costs are incurred.'

Maggie turned and started down the hall toward the steps that led to the first floor. She purposely left Rebecca and David to follow at a distance so that they might exchange their little confidences.

She didn't care about them. The water was clearing and she knew what position she would occupy in their little scheme of things. They would look upon her as a watchdog. The thought made her smile. They were so wrong. She would not try to keep them apart. On the contrary, she was pleased that they would be out of her hair, giving her free reign over the magnificent future that lay in store for her in Heather's house . . . *her* house now.

As they went down the stairs Maggie rummaged in her handbag and pulled out the receipts the freight-and-storage company had given her for their trunks. At the bottom of the stairs she turned, catching Rebecca and David with their heads bent close together, whispering as she knew they would.

'If you could arrange for these to be sent for,' she said, handing the receipts to David, 'I'd be most appreciative.'

'Of course,' he said.

Maggie pivoted and started out of the ugly white house. 'Come along, Rebecca,' she said as she tossed a glance over her shoulder. Then she hesitated and turned back again. 'Or would you prefer to accompany David this morning?'

Rebecca blushed, looking guilty again. 'No. Oh, no, Maggie. I'll . . . I'll come along with you . . . of course.'

Maggie smiled at David to show her authority over her sister. 'Put the cases on the back seat, David. We'll see you later at the house, I presume?' She was treating them like little children, but their romantic interlude was not what really troubled her. They'd both been in the upstairs bedroom last night — Rebecca had admitted as much — and both had had the opportunity to move that candelabrum. David was a stranger to her, but she knew Rebecca and what she was capable of.

As David piled the suitcases into the car, Maggie got directions to the grocery store. She reminded David first about the electricity, then the trunks, then the man to fix the window. She felt like a school-teacher assigning lessons. She enjoyed the authority. She felt so superior to Rebecca and David.

Mrs. Johnston was peeking through the

104

curtains, watching her ex-tenants depart. The old man in the wheelchair was sitting at the far end of the porch pretending to sleep, but Maggie saw his eyes peering at them from time to time.

Maggie turned toward the window behind which Mrs. Johnston stood. She purposely raised her hand and waved after the curtain fell back into place. Maggie knew Mrs. Johnston was spying on them; even this gave Maggie the additional pleasure of feeling better than people who spied and snooped and sneaked about.

She glanced toward the old man. 'Goodbye, Mr. Johnston,' she said pleasantly, just to let him know she knew he wasn't asleep. The old man didn't answer.

Before the morning ended the car was loaded up with bags and parcels and boxes of things Maggie bought. She and Rebecca spoke little during their shopping spree. With each item Maggie purchased she saw that Rebecca looked at her more and more disapprovingly, so she bought more than she intended just to show her sister that she had every intention of staying at

105

Heather House for a very long time.

Rebecca did not voice her disapproval until Maggie stopped at a furniture store and purchased a handsome and expensive high-fi unit encased in an extremely beautiful Spanish cabinet.

'But we have a hi-fi in storage,' Rebecca said.

'That's from my old life; this is for my new one. Besides, the old one isn't Spanish. It wouldn't fit into the living room decor,' Maggie told Rebecca.

'But golly, Maggie, it's so expensive.'

Maggie merely shrugged her shoulders. 'You spent some of your insurance money on the car and I said nothing, so kindly let me spend my money on what I want.'

From the furniture store they found a little music shop and Maggie bought several record albums, the most important of which to her was a complete recording of Chopin nocturnes. It was the same recording she and Rod had cherished all their lives. It made her somehow feel closer to him.

From the music shop they went to the bank, where Maggie arranged for a checking account. She also arranged for all her savings to be transferred from her old bank in the city.

'I'll want everything transferred here permanently,' Maggie told the bank's manager.

When he excused himself for a moment Rebecca leaned close and said, 'Aren't you going a little bit overboard? Why not leave your money where it's always been? Besides, the First City Bank pays a higher interest.'

'I obviously have no intention of ever returning to the city,' Maggie said. 'I see no reason to separate myself from my money. However, I presume that you think differently in view of the fact that you are not making a similar transfer of funds.'

'I'll open up a checking account for the amount of traveler's checks I brought. If I need more, Mr. Penticast at the First City Bank can arrange for it.'

'Then you are planning on going back?'

'Maybe not back,' Rebecca said, meeting Maggie's steady gaze. 'But I'm not all that convinced I'll be staying here.'

'And what does David have to say about you leaving your little love nest?'

'Really, Maggie. You're being perfectly dreadful.'

Maggie again shrugged and folded her hands complacently in her lap. Her newly found independence had given her the courage to open a personal checking account, not a joint one with Rebecca as had been the custom in the past. Let Rebecca fend for herself, Maggie thought. It was about time she did.

Rebecca, on the other hand, felt she was being punished for having spent the night in David's apartment. She had noticed that Maggie did not offer to open up a joint checking account, which they had always had. She did not protest. This was Maggie's way of showing her disapproval.

Rebecca had lived out Maggie's cool reproach in the past. After a few days things would change back again. Maggie would apologize for her harshness and things would be back to normal between them. Rebecca was prepared to ride out the storm. They'd been through things

108

like this before. Someday she would be rid of Maggie's childish moods, she thought. Someday.

The bank manager shook their hands and told them how pleased he was that they would be living in Pinebrook. He walked them to the door and bowed them out.

'Incidentally,' Maggie said to Rebecca when they were back in the car and heading toward Heather House, 'when we see David McCloud next, remind me that I want to talk to him about my buying the place.'

'Buying it? Oh, really, Maggie. Aren't you being just a bit hasty? You don't have the slightest idea of what Pinebrook and its people are like. How do you know you will want to live here? I realize you're purposely trying to be a bit spiteful for what I did last night, but . . . '

'What did you do last night, Rebecca?'

'You know what I'm referring to,' Rebecca said a bit shyly.

'What you do does not concern me,' Maggie said icily. 'That is, of course, unless it involves me directly.'

Rebecca gave her a wry look. 'You're being cute again, Maggie,' she sighed. 'I can't understand it. We always got along so well until we came here to this place. Ever since yesterday you've been acting like a different person.'

'I'm no different today than I was yesterday. Perhaps it's just that I'm letting my feelings come out into the open for once.'

Rebecca frowned at her. 'What's that supposed to mean?' Before Maggie had a chance to say anything Rebecca added, 'Are you saying you've felt this resentment toward me all these years, Maggie?'

Maggie could feel Rebecca's eyes boring into her profile. 'No, of course not,' she lied, but she felt her hands tightening on the steering wheel. She had felt resentment toward her sister and she was showing that resentment for the first time in her life. It almost felt good, although it made her slightly uneasy.

'What, then?' Rebecca persisted.

Maggie sighed. 'I think it's about time we both started living our own lives. We've been wrapped up in each other's affairs so tightly that we don't know which of us is which.'

Rebecca remembered something similar that David had said the previous night. She sat mulling it over in her mind.

They drove in silence for a while. Then Maggie said, 'Look, Rebecca,' as she turned and gave her sister a quick smile. 'I know you don't particularly like Heather House. I do. I like it very much. I want to live in it forever. I won't stand in your way if you choose to leave me here in Pinebrook. I won't be hurt or resent you for it. I just want us both to be happy. I believe I've found what will make me the happiest. Rod will come and we'll make Heather House one of the most beautiful places in the world.'

Rebecca was staring at her sister. She found herself frowning. She wondered if there was any possibility that Maggie was on the verge of a mental breakdown.

Maggie glanced at Rebecca again and she smiled. 'I see you are not going to try to convince me that Rod and George are dead.' She sighed. 'George may be, but I'm sure Rod is not.'

Rebecca said nothing.

'I take by your silence that you think I might be right.'

'I think nothing of the sort,' Rebecca said. 'George is dead and so is Rod.'

Although Rebecca's words came out firmly, there wasn't any conviction behind them. Maggie thought back, remembering the first time she began to believe that Rod was still alive. It was the day the insurance company delivered their very sizable checks. She'd told Rebecca that she really believed Rod to be dead. Rebecca had overreacted. Thinking back on that conversation, Maggie frowned. Was it possible that Rebecca, too, believed their husbands were still alive? The thought was most disturbing. Perhaps she knew something Maggie did not know.

'Surely you aren't serious about buying Heather House?' Rebecca asked. 'You can't mean to bury yourself out here in this hick town?'

'Wasn't it your idea we come here? Wasn't it you who leased this place for us?'

'But I never intended for us to live here the rest of our lives,' Rebecca said. 'I thought it would do us both good to get away from our friends and those old memories for a short while.'

Maggie kept her eyes fixed forward and her foot steady on the accelerator pedal. 'You needn't stay in Pinebrook. I have no chains on you, Rebecca. As for myself, I think I'll stay and wait for Rod.'

'You're crazy! Rod's dead, for God's sake. He's *dead*. Can't you get that through your skull?'

Maggie found herself smiling. 'Think me crazy if you wish, Rebecca, but somehow I am more convinced than ever that Rod's alive. He'll show up eventually, just you wait and see.'

Rebecca merely sat there, staring at her.

★   ★   ★

Sophie was coming down the stairs with a large cardboard box filled with burned debris. When she saw Maggie she stopped midway down. 'I was just cleaning up your room,' she said.

My room, Maggie thought with a wide, pleased grin. Sophie had said 'my' room, not 'the' room. Yes, she was home. She sighed and nodded to Sophie. 'Good girl. There'll be a workman here today, I hope, to fix the window.' She turned and started toward the kitchen. She turned back. 'Incidentally, Sophie, when the workman arrives tell him to check my bedroom door. It sticks.'

'Sticks?'

'Yes, it stuck last night; I couldn't open it.' Then she remembered the sound of laughter that she'd heard on the other side of that door. She felt a chill and it started her into thinking again about who had moved the candelabrum. She shook her head. She wouldn't think about anything unpleasant today.

'It works all right now,' Sophie said.

'Well, regardless,' Maggie said, dislodging her unpleasant thoughts, 'have the man check it when he comes.'

Rebecca must have come up behind Maggie. She didn't hear her but she saw Sophie's eyes move toward the front door. The girl looked at Rebecca in a strangely unfriendly way.

'The car's loaded with stuff, Sophie,'

Maggie said, secretly pleased at the look Sophie had cast at Rebecca. 'We'll put the groceries in the kitchen. You can put them away later, but I'd like you to show me where everything is.'

'Yes'm.'

Maggie noticed that Rebecca and Sophie did not greet each other, not even with a nod. That also pleased her.

Within the hour things were put away and Maggie and Rebecca had changed into housedresses. To Maggie's surprise Rebecca chose one of the large downstairs bedrooms for herself.

'But the room next to mine is lovely,' Maggie said.

'No, I think I'd prefer to sleep on the ground floor. Besides, it will give each of us more privacy.'

Then Maggie understood. Privacy, indeed. Rebecca would find it easier to sneak David in and out without Maggie knowing about it. Well, she'd handle that when the occasion arose. She had in the past.

'Have it your own way,' Maggie said with indifference. She smiled to herself, thinking that a new Maggie Garrison was

115

being born ... a Maggie Garrison Rebecca never knew and would obviously dislike. Rod had known, or had at least suspected, this new Maggie Garrison existed. She was sure he'd be pleased to find her when he came back.

The carpenter came. There was nothing wrong with the bedroom door. The window would take a lot of work, however. For the time being he measured and made sketches for the wood carving and glass work, then draped a white sheet over the gaping frame.

Maggie was upstairs hanging up her dresses when she heard a car drive up. She glanced out the window and saw that it was David, followed by a van from the power and light company. She went to the top of the stairs just as she heard Rebecca greet him.

'David, is that you?' Maggie called, not showing herself.

'Yes. Hi, Maggie. Everything going okay?'

'Yes, fine. Did you take care of everything?'

'Yes,' he called. 'Trunks have been sent for; the carpenter should be here already.'

'He's been and gone.'

116

'I had the electricity turned on. There's a man here now to check over the circuits.'

'Good. Are you staying for dinner?'

'Dinner? Do you think you're interested in having company already?'

'No trouble,' Maggie said.

Maggie heard David hesitate and was sure she'd heard whispering between him and Rebecca. Then David said, 'I have some things to clean up at the office. I can be back about seven if that's all right.'

'Great. See you at seven.'

Maggie left the head of the stairs without having shown herself at all. Let him see Rebecca in her housedress and low-heeled shoes, her hair in a bandana. Maggie had never really flirted with a man before, not even Rod (he had flirted with her), but she'd seen Rebecca do it often enough to know just how it was done. Tonight she'd do it. Tonight she'd give Rebecca a taste of her own medicine. The house was weaving its spell, having an influence on her, and she liked it very much.

As she went back into her room and

snapped shut the empty suitcase, she was thinking how wonderful it was to be alive. She went back out into the hall, looking for a storage room or any suitable place to keep her empty luggage. There was only one large hall closet and that was stacked with linens and towels and other odds and ends. Since Rebecca would not be using the other bedroom, Maggie decided to put her cases in the closet there.

Just as she stepped over the threshold she again smelled the faint hint of heather. She stopped in her tracks and sniffed the air. It was heather, there was no doubt about it. The room was dark, its drapes drawn closed. She went toward the windows and pulled back the curtains, letting the afternoon sun bring life to the room. As the room brightened the smell of heather seemed to dissipate.

Strange, she thought as she looked about the room. It was dusty and unkempt-looking. The bed was stripped and cobwebs hung from the ceiling. The windows hadn't been washed in years. Why had Sophie bothered to scour and scrub the big bed-room and not this one, knowing that both she and Rebecca would be sleeping here?

She didn't have long to ponder the question because she saw something else that made her thoughts deepen. There on the dusty night table next to the unmade bed was a bright, shiny key. It caught the rays of the sun and glinted back at her. She picked it up, noticing that there was no film of dust on it as there was on top of the night table. She ran her thumb over it. Her thumb came away clean. It was a large key, a door key, she decided. On impulse she carried it back out into the hall and fitted it into the lock of her bedroom door. The key turned easily, noiselessly, sending the bolt into place.

Her door hadn't stuck. It had been locked.

She felt the pulse in her temples begin to throb. Someone had locked her in the room last night after moving the candelabrum. Someone meant to do her harm. But who? And more important, *why?*

As she stood there in the hallway trying hard not to feel afraid, out of the corner of her eye she thought she saw movement. Something white and filmy fluttered out of sight down at the far end of the dim corridor.

'Sophie?' she called, but no one answered.

She unlocked the bedroom door she had just locked and pushed it open. Then she turned and started in the direction of where she thought she had seen movement. There was nothing there, she found, except the stairway — narrow and dark — leading up to the tower room. She started up them, remembering that David had said the stairs were unsafe, and testing each step as she went.

There was nothing wrong — that she could see — with the steps. They seemed in perfectly good condition . . . a bit dusty perhaps, but nonetheless in good repair.

The landing at the top had but one door. It was open. She went to the threshold.

'Sophie? Are you up here?'

No answer.

She stepped into the room, looking around. The room was beautiful. It was round, with windows looking in all directions. It was much larger than she had imagined it to be and furnished as a kind of bedroom-sitting room with a handsome bed draped in filmy lavender. The walls were a soft pink, the ceiling domed and carved like intricate French lace. A chaise longue was covered in rich purple and trimmed with cream-colored velvet. A thick fur rug, dyed the lightest shade of blue, covered the floor. Matching blue silk covered the occasional chairs. The furniture's wood was a warm brown; teak, Maggie thought.

The room had a strange, almost oriental flair, or perhaps like something out of the Arabian Nights. It brought back memories of childhood fairytales with the princess locked in the tower . . . of Rapunzel who lowered her hair so that her lover might climb it and rescue her; of black knights and white knights; of dragons and flying carpets.

Her romantic thoughts fled when she saw a pair of white gloves lying on the counterpane. There were her gloves. She picked them up and confirmed the monogram on the inside: M.G.

'Maggie Garrison,' she said aloud.

Somewhere far, far away, she thought she heard someone laugh.

6

Even with her clothes in the closet and a few personal appointments scattered around the room, Rebecca disliked the place. It was her fault that she was here; she admitted that. It had been her idea to get away from the city, and it had been her idea to come to Pinebrook after reading a description of this house in the real-estate section of the Sunday paper.

Heather House, as it was called, had seemed to be the answer to her prayers when David McCloud forwarded the photographs. It was uncanny, she thought, that a house could be so different in reality . . . so big, so formidable, so seemingly indestructible.

She had to stick it out, though. It had taken a lot of persuasion to get Maggie to pull up her roots and come here. She had managed, however, and she would see it all through somehow, even though she would have to force herself to make the

123

best of a bad situation.

Strange how things had made such a complete about-face. She blamed the house for that. Rebecca shook her head. She mustn't blame anyone or anything but herself for the predicament she was in. Besides, there was one redeeming feature about living here that she had not anticipated — David McCloud.

Memories of the night spent with him trickled back. She felt an all-over tingling sensation as she recalled the pleasure he'd given her. It was unfortunate that Maggie had found out about their all-night rendez-vous, but then Maggie always found out everything, and what she did not find out Rebecca always told her when it suited her.

Men were Rebecca's nemesis and she frankly admitted it. And if men were the strongest of her faults, truth was the strongest of her virtues. That was why everything seemed so difficult now. She knew all of her shortcomings and faced them without trying to delude herself or anyone else.

Was she living a lie by staying here with Maggie in Heather House? No, she didn't think she was. Maggie knew she wasn't happy with the house; that she was merely tolerating it. She'd bide her time here until the moment came to move on. And until that time came there was David to keep her amused and occupied.

Rebecca listened to the footsteps overhead. They sounded light and happy and she imagined Maggie humming to herself as she worked.

Maggie. How strange it was to realize that you could know someone the whole of their life and yet not know them at all. These past few days had brought out a different Maggie, a sister who was almost a stranger. The sweet, loving sister who'd cared for her all her life seemed to have vanished, and in her place was a cold, domineering woman who was determined to have things her way.

Rebecca shrugged. Why not? Maggie was entitled to her own life. The thing that upset her was the fact that this side of Maggie's personality had never manifested itself before. Maggie had kept it hidden deep inside all these years. It was Maggie who had lived a lie, if this new

Maggie was the true Maggie Garrison.

Or perhaps it wasn't the real Maggie she was seeing now. Perhaps it was merely a phase. Perhaps it only represented a flaw that she'd never recognized in her sister before. She remembered something Rod had said to her one time: most diamonds are imperfect. It held some comfort to know that Maggie was human after all and had flaws of her own.

Maggie had always done everything to ensure Rebecca's happiness; now she was trying to interfere with it. She had the right, Rebecca supposed as she wandered around the room, coming to rest at a window overlooking the garden patio.

Rebecca grimaced as she spotted a large fat-bellied lizard scoot up over the root of a cactus plant and settle itself in the sun atop a flat rock. It lay there motionless, letting itself melt into its surroundings until it became invisible. She looked away, and when she looked back she could not find the slithering little creature. Having seen it, however, she imagined the place being alive with such odious, crawling things.

'Rebecca.'

She turned and found Maggie standing in the doorway. Rebecca was surprised to see that Maggie wasn't the happy, humming, smiling girl she'd pictured trotting about upstairs.

Maggie walked toward her carrying a pair of white gloves in her hand.

Rebecca grinned. 'You're hardly dressed for white gloves,' she said. 'They don't go very well with that saggy old housedress and those work shoes.'

'I found these up in the tower room.'

'I thought David said it wasn't safe to go up there.'

Maggie made a face to show that she did not put much importance in anything David said or would say. 'I laid these beside my purse on the table in the living room last night. They disappeared. I just found them up in the tower.'

'Sophie most likely was playing around with them.'

'Sophie wasn't home last night. She was at a Halloween party at the church.'

'Then she borrowed them this morning.'

Maggie frowned down at the gloves. 'No, they were missing last night. I looked for them.'

'Maybe it was the ghost,' Rebecca said with a laugh. She saw that Maggie wasn't amused, however.

'You have a pair just like these, don't you?'

'You know I do,' Rebecca said. 'You gave them to me. You bought both pairs at the same time, if I remember correctly.'

'Where are yours?'

Rebecca reached out and took the gloves from Maggie's hand. 'These are yours, Mag. Your monogram is on the inside.'

'I know,' Maggie said, sounding a little impatient. 'You do have yours, don't you?'

'Of course,' Rebecca answered, looking a bit mystified. 'They are over there in my bag. I wore them last night.'

Maggie moved toward the handbag and snapped it open. She pulled out the pair of white gloves that were tucked in one corner. She flattened them in her hand, turning them over. She did not know what was pressing her on to examine the gloves, but when she did her fingers

128

touched hard little drops of wax encrusted on the right-hand glove. She tested the wax drops with her nail. A tightening feeling crept over her.

'There's wax on them,' she said softly, almost fearing to say the words.

'So there's wax on them. I may have been fiddling with the candles on the table in the restaurant.' She flushed slightly. 'David lit candles in his apartment last night. I may have put them down nearby.'

Maggie tossed the gloves down as though they were contaminated. There hadn't been any candles on the table in the restaurant and she doubted if David McCloud was the type of man to burn candles in his room during a sexual interlude. She had a dreadful fear that she knew how the wax got on Rebecca's glove. She did not want to face the realization but the proof was there, hardened on the soft, white fabric, and she could not ignore it.

'Why did you do it, Rebecca?' Maggie turned slowly and fixed her eyes solidly on her sister's.

'Do what? What are you talking about?'

129

'You know perfectly well what I'm talking about. You came into my bedroom upstairs and moved the candelabrum. You set fire to the room. I want to know why.'

'Are you insane? In God's name, why would I want to do a thing like that? Maggie, you must be mad to even suspect I could set fire to a room with you asleep inside it. What kind of a monster do you think I am? Surely you know me well enough by now to know I'd be incapable of such a thing.'

'It wouldn't be the first time.'

'Good God, Maggie! That was almost twenty years ago. I've changed; you know that.'

'I don't think I know anything of the sort, Rebecca. I don't think I've ever known you at all.'

'Nor I you,' Rebecca flared. 'I don't know what the devil has gotten into you these past few days, but whatever it is, I don't like it.'

'And so you tried to set fire to me?'

'Maggie!' They stood glowering at each other. 'If you weren't my sister I'd slap your face for that crack. How dare you

130

insinuate such a thing?'

'Because there's wax on your glove. You were in this house last night. You were in my room and knew I was asleep there.'

'So there's wax on my glove. That doesn't mean I tried to burn you alive. And as for being in this house last night, I wasn't the only one here.'

Maggie tilted up her head and eyed her sister with cold suspicion. 'What do you mean?'

'Well, Sophie could have been here before or during her party. David was here with me. And someone else.'

'Someone else?'

'Yes. We heard someone's car start up after we left the house and parked in the grove to admire the scenery.'

'Whose car?'

'How should I know? I don't know anybody around here.'

'What kind of a car was it?'

'I don't know that, either.' She hesitated, looking embarrassed. 'If you must know, we were too busy necking to turn and look at it when it passed on the road.'

Maggie tried to sort out this new bit of

information. One more suspect was something she had not counted upon.

'Maggie, ever since we came to this house you have been acting so strangely I don't know you. Do you truly think I was responsible for the fire in your room last night?' When Maggie did not answer, Rebecca went over to her and shook her. 'Do you really think that?'

Slowly Maggie raised her eyes again. She looked deep into her sister's eyes, refusing to let her gaze falter again. 'I don't know, Rebecca. I just do not know.'

She turned stiffly and started out of the room, scooping up her gloves that Rebecca had laid down on the table. At the door she paused. Sounding as unruffled as though they had spoken nothing but pleasantries for the past several minutes, Maggie said, 'David is coming for dinner. I suggest you get straightened up. I'll take care of the cooking so you needn't bother with anyone or anything but yourself.'

As she went back up the stairs, Maggie made a mental line-up of all those on her suspect list. There was Sophie, of course, who was so irresponsible she might be capable of just about anything. Then there was David McCloud . . . and her sister, Rebecca . . . and someone else, someone who'd driven to Heather House last night.

None of it made sense. Only Rebecca had any reason to wish her ill. But, to see her dead? What could Rebecca gain by that? There was only the money that remained from Rod's insurance. It was a sizable sum, true, but not sizable enough to kill for. Besides, Rebecca had money of her own and she was young enough to remarry or earn more. And Rebecca surely wasn't capable of it now. The doctor said . . .

Maybe the doctor was wrong.

The past started to crowd in on her. She shook her head. 'No,' she said, 'that was a long time ago.'

David had no reason to want her dead. Sophie, of course, was unbalanced; there was no doubt about that. Maggie would have to be on her guard where Sophie was concerned. But even Sophie wouldn't burn down the roof over her own head.

And who had driven past Rebecca and

David in the grove? Maggie didn't know anyone in Pinebrook who'd want to see her dead, but then she didn't know who was living in Pinebrook. Perhaps there was someone from her past who'd seen her and learned she was going to be living at Heather House. That, too, was silly because there wasn't a single person in her past who would benefit from her death.

Suddenly Maggie saw Rod and Rebecca wrapped in a heated embrace. Rod was alive, she'd always known that. He hadn't drowned in that accident. A wife could feel such things as a husband's death. She'd never believed or accepted the news of Rod's death, and never would believe it until she saw his lifeless body for herself. The reason the insurance people hadn't found the bodies was because there were no bodies to find. She'd thought about that for a long, long time.

She started climbing the steps again . . . very slowly.

Rebecca was the one who had accidentally found this house listed for rent in the real-estate section of the paper. Rebecca

134

was the one who had insisted they come here to live. Was it possible that Rebecca knew Rod was alive? Was it Rod who'd driven away from Heather House last night? Was this all some bizarre plot to unite her husband and her sister?

Rebecca had overreacted when Maggie mentioned her suspicion that Rod was not dead. Rod could well be living somewhere in Pinebrook, waiting for the chance to get Maggie out of the way. It was possible that Rebecca had managed to turn him against Maggie.

She pushed her hands back through her hair. Oh God, no. It just could not be. She was thinking like a madwoman. Rod wasn't capable of such a horrible thing; neither was Rebecca. Not really.

She found herself standing at the window of her room, looking out. She glanced at a frail little sparrow struggling with a huge twig which was obviously too heavy for it to carry away. A second sparrow, just as tiny and frail-looking, fluttered down. Between them they caught the twig in their beaks and flew off with it.

Maggie buried her face in her hands.

7

All her designs for seducing David were tarnished now by her new suspicions. As sure as she was that Rod was still alive, she was just as convinced that David McCloud was playing a part in whatever scheme was afoot.

Maggie was sitting before her dressing table looking not at her reflection, but the ghost shadows beyond it. She got up and wandered about the bedroom. The moment her mind's eye was taken from the figures in the mirror, the room took over the scene. She hugged herself, feeling the solid security the walls and floors and ceiling radiated. Nothing could harm her so long as she stayed here in Heather House.

She would have to get Rebecca away somehow, preferably with David McCloud. With Rebecca running off with David, Rod would see the folly of his ways and return here to her and to Heather House.

She'd play along with their little game, but she and Heather House would remain victorious. Rebecca had tempted Rod away; Maggie would tempt him back again. Regardless of his faults, she knew he was the only man she could ever love.

She glanced back into the mirror. Suddenly the shadows faded and her face's reflection took shape before her eyes. She had to look closely in order to recognize herself. She was different. More beautiful. The lines at the corners of her eyes seemed less pronounced and there was a certain fullness about the mouth that she was pleased to see. A new kind of softness surrounded her features — a mature, refined loveliness that she liked.

She knew she'd left the old Maggie Garrison back in her old life and the new one was much more to her liking, both in attitude and looks. She was thinking differently, acting differently, looking differently. She felt more alive and stronger, more capable . . . and more selfish, she added, feeling a bit guilty.

She went to the full-length mirror near the bed and examined the overall picture she intended to present downstairs. Her hair piled high gave her a regal bearing. She tilted up her chin and smiled with satisfaction at what she saw in the glass.

She'd never wear a black dress again. The flowing maroon dinner gown accentuated the darkness of her hair, the darkness of her eyes. It flattered her features. The single strand of pearls was in perfect taste. Rebecca, she knew, would bedeck herself with too much jewelry that clanked and jangled whenever she moved, calling attention to herself. Quiet sophistication wins out over flamboyancy every time, Maggie reminded herself. Like fireworks, flashes and bursts of color attract every eye; but the attraction is not long-lasting, merely a fleeting thing. The plain, soft, restful beauty of the night sky they explode against is what everyone finds far more comfortable and relaxing.

She heard David's car pull into the driveway. She was ready. She knew what she was going to do. She heard Rebecca call, 'David's here.'

'Coming.'

Maggie went to the top of the stairs

138

and stood in the curve of the landing, out of sight. She heard Rebecca go across the foyer and open the door.

'Hi.'

'Hi.'

And then there was a pause. They were embracing, Maggie knew. She waited.

'Hey,' she heard David say after a moment. 'I see you decided to go along with the other Pinebrook residents.'

'What do you mean?' Rebecca asked.

'Your door. You've painted it white, I see.'

There was the opening and closing of the door again and Rebecca said, 'I hadn't noticed. I thought it had always been painted white.'

Maggie started down then. 'I asked the carpenter to paint it for me when he was here this afternoon,' she said.

They both turned. It was easy to see that David had not heard a single word of what she'd said. He was staring at her, drinking in her beauty. The look in his eyes assured her that her plan would work nicely.

'Absolutely ravishing,' he gushed as he

came quickly to the bottom of the stairs, leaving Rebecca standing at the open front door. 'Maggie Garrison, you are a knockout,' he said with a handsome grin on his face.

'Thank you, kind sir.'

Rebecca, too, was staring at her. 'Maggie, you're beautiful,' she said admiringly. 'Where on earth have you been hiding that dress? And your hair. Why haven't you worn it like that before?'

David took her hand and pressed it to his lips. 'Your servant, ma'am.'

'You may fix me a drink, kind sir,' she chided back. 'One vodka martini in a thin-stemmed glass, very cold, very dry and with a twist of lemon peel, please.'

'You have but to command. Where's the hooch?' He laughed gaily and went toward the living room. At the doorway he turned. 'How about you, Rebecca?' he asked, making it sound a little like an afterthought. Maggie saw the tiny little crease appear and disappear on her sister's forehead.

'The same,' Rebecca said. She closed the front door and put her arm around

Maggie's waist. Maggie could tell it was a forced gesture. 'You've never looked more beautiful, Maggie,' Rebecca said, giving her sister a squeeze. That, too, was artificial, Maggie decided. 'You were wise to hide that dress before I could get my hands on it. Where on earth did you get it? And when?'

Maggie felt confident. She let herself talk girl-talk until David produced the martinis, then she turned her attention completely to him. She would make Rebecca jealous, which wasn't altogether difficult to do. It was one of her sister's several weaknesses. Being jealous, Rebecca always acted too hastily, moved and reacted too carelessly. She would react out of spite and Maggie knew that more often than not, poor, jaundiced Rebecca usually wound up spiting herself.

They lingered over the cocktails but Maggie purposely excused herself every so often, saying she had to check with Sophie to make sure dinner was being prepared according to Maggie's instructions.

Sophie needed no help, of course; Maggie used the ploy to show herself off

141

to her best advantage, gliding gracefully across the living room, leaving a delicious hint of her favorite perfume trailing in her wake. Rebecca, she knew, was content to keep herself curled up like a kitten, diminishing herself into a little-girl size close to David's side. A moving object attracts much more attention than an immobile one, Maggie concluded.

Her efforts were rewarded. Each time she left or entered the room David's eyes were on her. He'd comment about how delicious the food smelled, or he would remark about how well the new hi-fi unit blended into the decor of the room, but his thoughts were definitely not on his words . . . They were on Maggie.

'How old is this house?' Maggie asked David just as Rebecca started to say something about how little she knew about wines and grapes. Maggie knew just as little but would never admit it to anyone, especially a man who was more or less a connoisseur, as David claimed to be.

'Quite old, believe it or not,' he said, smiling.

'I believe it,' Rebecca said out of the corner of her mouth.

'But *how* old?' Maggie persisted.

David wrinkled his brow and started to think. 'Well, I believe it was built sometime before the turn of the century. Offhand I'd say it was about a hundred years old, give or take a few years.'

Rebecca made a face. 'No wonder it's falling apart.'

Maggie flashed a bright, indulgent smile. 'Oh, Rebecca, how can you say that? This place is like a citadel. I see nothing of deterioration here.'

David leaned forward, resting his elbows on his knees and twirling his cocktail glass between his palms. 'Structurally, this house could stand for another hundred years,' he said. 'We had some fellows go over it from top to bottom just recently. They passed it with flying colors.' He looked around the room. 'No, they don't build houses like this anymore.'

'I still think it's like living in a bank vault.'

'Rebecca, you're just not romantic,' Maggie said slyly. Her head felt light and her feet seemed not to be anchored to the floor. She reveled in the weightlessness of her body. Yet, despite the slight giddiness she felt, her thoughts stayed very cool and very rational.

A large painting hung on one wall, of a man standing proud and erect beside a handsome, carved Spanish table. She'd seen the painting earlier, of course, and had admired it greatly. She'd seen the Spanish table as well; it was in the room David had referred to as the library.

'Who's that? Did he build this house?'

'No, that's Heather Lambert's husband, Louis Michael Lambert the Third. Quite an impressive fellow, wouldn't you say?'

'Very,' Maggie agreed. She glanced around at the other paintings. 'Isn't there a portrait of Heather Lambert, too?'

'There used to be,' David said. 'My father tells me they had their portraits painted at the same time and had a lavish party to celebrate their unveiling. Her portrait used to hang opposite his . . . over there where that large landscape now hangs. Whatever happened to it, or why she had it taken down, nobody seems to know.

People who knew them and came here said that it was Heather's ghost who took down the painting. It was hanging on that wall when she died.'

'What did she die of?' Rebecca asked.

David shrugged. 'A broken heart, everyone said.'

Maggie sighed. 'Like poor Isolde.' She walked back and stood before Louis Lambert's portrait. She studied it for a moment. 'What a curious ring he's wearing on his finger. Isn't it a bit flowery for a man?'

David laughed. 'According to gossip, Heather had that ring designed to look like a sprig of heather. In the very center of the design she had her name engraved so that he'd never forget her. I suppose she always suspected he'd run off and leave her one day.'

'Was he that kind of man?'

'They say he was.'

'The cad,' Maggie said with a smile. 'How could he leave such a wonderful house as this? I just love it here.' She strolled around the room, admiring the old portraits, running an idle finger across

145

the top of a table or a cabinet. 'You know,' she started, 'I've never been so affected by a house before.'

'I'm all for going out and conquering the world,' Rebecca said as she drained her glass and handed it to David to refill. Maggie saw her smile and saw the way she let her fingers linger on David's hand. 'Anything, just so long as it gets us out of here.'

'I for one would hate to see you go anywhere,' David said. He was talking to Rebecca but his eyes were on Maggie. He filled Rebecca's glass and handed it to her. 'Maggie?'

'Oh, no, thank you, David. I'm afraid vodka and I become enemies after one glass.'

'Since when?' Rebecca took a deep swallow.

'How about some music?' David said. 'I'd like to hear your new set.'

'Oh, how silly of me,' Maggie said as she went over and switched it on. The soft, lovely strains of a popular song drifted over the room. 'I'm not all that proficient at entertaining gentlemen. A

146

more experienced hostess would have had the music playing before you arrived. You should have reminded me about the music, Rebecca.'

'You're an admirable hostess,' David said. 'Would you care to dance?'

Maggie smiled as his arms went around her and they started a fox trot. She could feel Rebecca's eyes on her back. She let her arm go up around David's neck, moving her body closer to his.

'You dance very well,' he said, smiling down into her upturned face.

'Maggie does everything very well,' Rebecca said from the couch.

'You are both too flattering,' Maggie said, but she knew that Rebecca had not intended her remark to be flattering. Too often in the past it had been she on the couch and Rebecca in the arms of the man, dancing closely, whispering, smiling, flirting. Too many times Maggie had watched Rebecca dance with Rod while she sat and listened to George talk about his problems at work. Those days were finished.

Just as the dance music ended, Sophie

appeared in the doorway and motioned to Maggie.

'Sophie is ready to start serving dinner,' Maggie said, easing herself out of David's arms. She felt the reluctance with which he released her. She smiled up at him and patted his arm. 'Shall we go in?'

The dining room was lighted by a trio of candelabra placed down the center of the long oak table. In the muted light the room looked enchanting. Maggie herself had arranged two lovely silver bowls of flowers on the table and a large spray that dominated the serving cabinet. Yellows and oranges and lush, bright greens gave a delicate airiness to the room that complemented the heavy strength of the furniture.

'I've set the three places together at this end,' Maggie explained. 'I thought it would be much more intimate than spreading us out. This table could easily accommodate twelve quite comfortably.'

'Twenty-four,' David corrected as they settled themselves.

Maggie gave him an astonished look.

'My parents used to come here, I've been told. They used to talk quite frequently about Heather Lambert's lavish dinner parties.'

Rebecca gave her attention to the soup. Maggie could see she was annoyed.

Maggie cocked her head at David. 'I don't know where I got the impression that Heather Lambert was more or less a recluse.'

'Oh, not until after her husband disappeared. In her earlier days this house was a regular mecca for parties and balls and dinners. My father tells me that Heather Lambert was one of the most beautiful women he'd ever seen. Of course, I'm prejudiced toward my own generation; I don't think Heather Lambert could hold a candle to you.' He looked over at Rebecca. 'Or you,' he added.

'Who lived here before the Lamberts?' Maggie asked.

'Heather's parents. Her family built the house. Her husband's name was Lambert. Heather's maiden name was Alquarez. She was a dark-haired, dark-eyed, fiery Latin beauty with the complexion of creamy ivory.'

'And a heart of blue steel,' Rebecca

commented in between spoonfuls of soup.

'Why do you say that?' Maggie asked, glancing at her sister.

Rebecca shrugged. 'Just this house, I guess. I get the impression that only a very cold and calculating woman would enjoy an atmosphere like this.' She kept her eyes leveled straight at Maggie.

'We are all quite aware, Rebecca dear, that you do not seem to favor this place. You needn't remind us at each and every turn of the conversation.'

David cleared his throat. 'The soup is heaven. Did Sophie make it?'

'No, I did,' Maggie said.

Sophie appeared to clear away the first course. She had a disturbed, almost frightened expression on her face. When Maggie noticed it she asked, 'Is anything wrong, Sophie?'

'Miss Heather says somebody took her gloves.'

'I beg your pardon?'

Maggie saw quick glances exchanged between Sophie and David. 'Nothing,' Sophie grunted as she piled the soup plates one on top of the other and went out of the room.

When the swinging door closed Rebecca said, 'She said, 'Miss Heather says somebody took her gloves,' whatever that means. That one's a bit off the deep end, if you ask me.'

Sophie came back in carrying the next course. Everyone remained silent until she was out of the room again.

'She's perfectly harmless,' David said. 'Poor Sophie has just refused to believe her mistress is gone. She idolized her.'

Before any of them could touch the fish the door swung open again and Sophie appeared, but briefly. She just poked her head into the dining room. Her eyes were on fire. 'Whoever took them better give them back. She's really mad.' The door swung shut.

In the dead silence that followed it started. The ice cubes in the tall water goblets began to rattle against the sides of the glasses. The prisms of the overhead chandelier began to tinkle like wind chimes heralding a storm.

The bases of the candelabra thumped

and the floral centerpieces inched this way and that on the table.

'What in heaven's name?' Maggie exclaimed.

The whole room began to tremble. The floor beneath their feet shook. A low rumbling sound, like that of distant thunder, got louder and louder.

'Earthquake!' David shouted. 'Quick, under the table!'

They threw themselves down.

Deep in the recesses of the house someone screamed.

The three were huddled together, stiff as figures in a painting, waiting for the rumbling noise to stop and for the house to settle. When all went quiet David, as though coming alive, got slowly to his feet. The others followed suit.

'I think it's over,' he said as he headed toward where he thought the scream had come from. Maggie and Rebecca were close at his heels. 'It's a good thing you ladies are from around these parts. Easterners just can't cope with our little earth tremors.'

'Do you think that's what it was?'

Rebecca asked anxiously.

'What else could it have been?' Maggie said.

They pushed their way through the butler's pantry and out into the kitchen. Sophie was on the floor, seemingly cowering near the big stove.

'Are you all right, Sophie?' Maggie asked, rushing over to her. She went to lay her hand on Sophie's arm, but before she touched her she gasped. She saw the blank stare, the sagging mouth.

'Oh, my God!' Maggie gasped. 'She's dead!'

8

She scarcely knew Sophie, yet the sight of her frail little body being lifted onto the stretcher and carried out to the waiting ambulance brought tears to Maggie's eyes. She couldn't decide if they were tears of grief or of fear. There was a stabbing in her breast and a voice kept telling her that Mrs. Johnston had been right after all. Heather House was evil; she must get away from it.

But another voice told her that wherever she went this evil would follow her. It wasn't Heather House that had bludgeoned the life out of Sophie; it was someone in the house.

But who? Maggie asked herself.

★   ★   ★

After the police photographer and forensic investigators had descended on the kitchen where Sophie's body had been

154

found, and other officers began to search the house and grounds, David, Maggie and Rebecca had all been separately interviewed and questioned. Later both had been driven to a police station, with David being allowed to drive his own car there, accompanied by a police officer.

At the station they were asked to sign statements that had been prepared from their earlier interviews. The police had told Maggie that she would not be able to return to Heather House until the forensic investigations had been carried out, but they were informed that they could return after midday the following day. Maggie had refused the offer of police protection, and so had Rebecca — somewhat to Maggie's surprise.

Overnight accommodation was provided for Maggie and Rebecca at the station, but David was allowed to return to his lodging at Mrs. Johnston's. He left with the promise that he would return for them at midday. Maggie smiled to herself at Rebecca's expression as David took his leave. Clearly she would have liked to accompany him, but had decided that it would be embarrassing with the police drawing their conclusions.

* * *

As Maggie re-entered Heather House, she felt Rebecca's arm go around her.

'Don't think about what's happened, Maggie. As the policeman said, it must have been a prowler or some horribly demented vagrant who Sophie had taken in.'

'Why would anyone want to kill Sophie? It makes no sense,' David said.

'Nothing makes any sense anymore,' Maggie answered, her mind wandering back over the past year.

Rebecca hugged her. 'Come on, Maggie. Let's pack a few things and then get out of here.'

'And go where?'

'Any place but here.'

Maggie shook her head. 'I couldn't face that house of Mrs. Johnston's. Besides, the police told us they'd searched the house. They found tire tracks leading

156

away from the wooded area at the back. Whoever killed Sophie won't be back, I'm sure.'

'But the place is giving me the willies. I've got to get out of it, at least for a little while,' Rebecca said.

David touched Maggie's arm. 'Rebecca's right. Let's take a drive. At least a change of scenery will help. What do you say?'

Again Maggie shook her head. 'No, you two go along if you want to. There's so much to straighten up.' She let her eyes wander toward the kitchen.

'Don't you dare go into that kitchen, Maggie,' Rebecca said firmly. 'I forbid it. You're upset enough.'

'Please, Rebecca,' Maggie said, regaining her composure. 'I am not a child. I think I'd like very much to be left alone. You and David go for a drive if you wish. I just want to be alone and think.'

'Alone? In this house? Over my dead body,' Rebecca said.

Maggie turned to David. 'Take Rebecca for a drive, David. She's more upset than I am, although she doesn't want to show it. I'll be fine, really I will.'

157

'I'm sorry, Maggie, but I think Rebecca's right. You mustn't stay alone in this house. You should get out of here, at least for an hour or so.'

'No,' Maggie said. 'Whoever killed Sophie is far gone by now.' What she didn't say was she was certain there was some evidence the police might have overlooked that would give her a clue as to who that someone was. She had a good idea of who, but the thought was so disturbing she didn't want to think about it. Yet, she had to be sure her suspicions were correct. She had to search the house and find out whatever she could without Rebecca or David being there, spying on her.

'Go along, you two,' Maggie insisted. 'I'll be fine.'

She went up the stairs quickly and closed the door of her bedroom. She waited until she heard David's car drive off, then she came out of the room and went back downstairs. Without hesitating she went directly toward the kitchen. If she came face to face with him she was certain she had nothing to fear. She could talk to

158

him, reason with him as she had done so often in the past.

Maggie didn't feel afraid. He loved her; he meant her no harm.

There was no one in the kitchen when she got there; the cellar door, however, was ajar.

As she touched the knob a strange, peppery odor caught in her nostrils. She pulled the door open. The odor sharpened. Maggie thought about the smell of heather she'd experienced the night before. It wasn't heather this time; it was much too pungent to be anything as pleasant as that.

Maggie searched for a light switch. There wasn't any. Of course there wasn't, she told herself, remembering the police with their flashlights. She turned back and took an old kerosene lamp down from its nail. She stood at the top of the stairs, looking down into the dark, dusty cavern of the cellar. There was nothing to be afraid of, she kept telling herself.

The cellar was strangely warm, with a close, smothering atmosphere. She was forced to breathe through her mouth to

159

get rid of the biting sensation in her nostrils. Something thin and wispy trailed across her face and she gave a little gasp. The cord from a light socket hung in front of her eyes. She yanked at it but nothing happened. She would make a point of replacing the bulb tomorrow. The thought made her pause.

Maggie hadn't prowled through many cellars and the sensation was a strange one. It was like walking through a tunnel that had no end. She saw the crates and trunks and wondered what long-past memories and secrets were locked up inside them. Possibly clothes from bygone days worn by people who were long since dead and in their graves. Perhaps collections of love letters, Heather Lambert's love letters, tied neatly with ribbons and laid lovingly to rest.

The peppery smell became more pronounced. It seemed to come from the direction of the far wall.

At the far wall Maggie found nothing but solid brick and stone encrusted with dirt and dust. The wall felt rough when she touched it. She reveled in its solidity, the firmness of its texture. The roots of Heather House, she thought, so deep and secure, so unyielding. Nothing, not even nature's cruelties, would ever represent a threat to this foundation. She wanted to press herself against this buttress, this bulwark, and make herself one with it. It was the strength she'd never had.

As she moved along, her hand bumped against something less solid that was leaning against the wall. Maggie held her lantern up close to it. It was flat and rectangular in shape, draped with a thick canvas which was layered with dust. On impulse she pulled away the canvas.

Clouds of dust swirled up and over her. She began to cough, groping for a handkerchief to cover her nose and mouth. Her coughing spasm almost caused the lantern to fall from her hand. She set it carefully on the floor and fanned the air to clear the swirling dust. She stepped back and waited for the gray, powdery grime to settle.

Gradually there materialized before Maggie's eyes a portrait of a woman dressed all in white, holding a small

161

bouquet of what was unmistakably heather. Maggie stared at the bouquet for a moment, then slowly raised her eyes to the face.

'Heather Lambert,' she said aloud.

The name came to her spontaneously. She had never seen Heather Lambert, nor had she ever heard a description of her other than the sketchy one David had given; yet she knew instinctively that this was a portrait of Heather Lambert, mistress of Heather House. This was the portrait that had been taken down from the wall of the living room.

Maggie had never seen a more beautiful woman. Her hair was dark as a raven's, hanging long and loose over her naked shoulders. The creamy whiteness of her dress brought out a smoldering of the eyes. Her long, delicate fingers encircled the stems of the bouquet of heather, which was painted in such exquisite detail that Maggie almost mistook the acrid smell in the cellar for the heather in the painting.

She stood there gazing up at the exquisite features of the woman and thought the artist must indeed have been very much in love with her. Every man must have been in love with her, Maggie thought. How could they not be? She was the loveliest woman Maggie had ever seen. And yet her husband had abandoned her. How could he?

Maggie's eyes noticed the handsome gilt frame around the canvas. The frame and the portrait itself were in perfect condition. Why, then, was it buried down here in this murky old cellar? Why had someone draped it in canvas to hide it from the appreciative eyes of the rest of the world? It was a masterpiece. She couldn't possibly let it remain down here. It belonged in a place of honor, a place where everyone could enjoy the exquisite beauty of Heather Alquarez Lambert.

Maggie had trouble lifting the painting, as it was large and heavy and awkward to maneuver. She glanced down toward the floor where she'd placed the lantern. The beams of light illuminated the dust and dirt on the floor and Maggie frowned, noticing that she wasn't the first to have tried to move the painting. The ground was scuffed. It appeared that the painting had been pushed or dragged away from the wall, and rather recently, because the floor looked newly scratched.

She tried lifting the painting but it was far too wide and much too tall for her to grasp. It threatened to tumble down on her. She'd have to wait and get Rebecca or David to help her with it in the morning.

As Maggie struggled to put the portrait back against the wall something black and jagged caught her eye. She picked up the lantern, eased the portrait forward silently and peered behind it. The smell, strong and peppery, was intense. It was oozing from a large, gaping hole that had apparently been blasted into the lower part of the wall. She felt the ragged edges of bricks.

Someone must have recently tried to blow away a section of the wall. She could not fit herself behind the portrait and was afraid she'd knock it forward and deface it if she tried. She attempted to push it aside but something was holding it fast. When she investigated she found that a pile of bricks had been knocked to one side, butting up against the frame of the portrait.

She stood there staring down at the rubble. What could it mean? Who had pushed aside the portrait of Heather Lambert and had tried to blast a hole in the brick wall, and for what reason? Maggie rubbed an idle finger across her chin. Her nostrils stung from the sharpness of the smell. The explosion had been recent.

Then another thought grabbed her mind. There had been no earthquake! Someone had been in the cellar, had moved the painting and had set off a charge. Sophie had obviously seen whoever it was. Someone had come down here carrying some kind of charge and had detonated it, shaking the house. But why?

Maggie remembered the fire in her bedroom. Had someone tried to burn her out, and, having failed that, was now trying to blow her up? No, Maggie was sure Rebecca was responsible for the fire. She remembered the gloves with the hardened wax and she remembered something similar happening a long time ago.

Rod? Had he crept down here? A man could easily have managed moving the portrait. No, it couldn't have been Rod, not if her suspicions were correct. Rod would not chance blowing up the house with Rebecca inside it. And David . . . ?

Maggie reached behind the portrait again, groping around the opening. Several of the surface bricks had been blasted away near the bottom, leaving a gaping black hole. The charge had only succeeded in knocking away part of the wall and weakening it.

If someone had taken the time and trouble to blow a hole in the wall, whoever it was would surely be back to finish the job. No one had intended to blow up the house; that could easily have been accomplished by simply using a bigger, more devastating type of explosive. No, there was obviously something behind the wall — or under it — that someone desperately wanted.

Why had anyone tried last night when

it was obvious there were people in the house? Certainly whoever it was had seen the cars parked in the driveway, had seen the lights, had heard the voices and the music. Maggie pondered that for a moment. Of course! Before yesterday there hadn't been any need to remove whatever was being searched for because there had not been anyone living in the house prior to then, only harmless old Sophie.

'That has to be it,' she said aloud, proud that she had finally solved this part of the puzzle. She glanced again behind the portrait. Someone knew something was hidden under or behind the bricks and had to get it out before anyone else discovered it. Someone afraid the new tenants might renovate the place from attic to cellar and discover something damaging. What?

She returned to the kitchen and made herself a meal, then spent the rest of the afternoon looking about the house, but did not discover anything of significance. She had not been able to sleep very well in her uncomfortable bed at the police station, and when she sat down on the settee she drifted off to sleep.

She awoke to find it was evening. She felt refreshed, and decided to take another look at Heather Lambert's picture. It held an uncanny fascination for her.

She had only been in the cellar a few minutes when overhead she heard a door slam shut. She lifted the lantern and peered up again into the face of Heather Lambert. The face seemed to be smiling at her. There was something about the expression on the face of the painting that told her she was right. Woman's instinct, premonition, call it what you will, Maggie knew she was thinking along the correct lines.

She almost felt like laughing. They wouldn't trick her. Nobody would trick Maggie Garrison. The intelligence of Heather House was offering itself to her and as a team they could not fail.

'We'll wait them out,' she found herself saying up into Heather's painted face. She didn't quite understand why she'd said that, but it seemed right to say it to this beautiful woman, standing so tall and regal in her gilt frame.

Footsteps sounded overhead, walking across the kitchen floor. Rebecca was back earlier than she'd expected. She'd worked faster than Maggie thought she would.

'Maggie! Are you down there?' Rebecca called.

'I'm coming,' she called back.

She turned and looked up at Heather Lambert. 'We'll wait,' she whispered, and then turned and hurried out of the cellar.

She'd wait for tomorrow.

9

'Why did you turn off all of the lights?' Rebecca asked when Maggie emerged from the cellar. 'Had you expected me to stay at David's?'

At a glance Maggie could tell she was upset, and it wasn't over Sophie's death. Rebecca, contrary to what Maggie told David, never got upset over anything unless it concerned herself personally.

'I didn't turn off the lights,' Maggie said. She blew out the lantern and replaced it on its nail.

'The lights were off when David drove me back . . . except for that weird light in the tower.'

'So they were off,' Maggie said flippantly. 'What does it matter? A woman was killed in this house tonight and you're concerned about lights being turned off.'

'And what on earth were you doing in that dreary old cellar? Just look at your beautiful dress. It's ruined.'

'It is not ruined,' Maggie answered, brushing it off with her hands. 'It can easily be cleaned. It's only dust.'

'Good heavens, Maggie. What were you doing down there? After what happened in this house last night I can't understand how . . . '

'I'd prefer to forget what happened here last night. I don't want to think about it.'

Rebecca eyed her brazenly. 'Are you referring to Sophie's death or the disgusting way you threw yourself at David yesterday?'

'Did I throw myself at David? Funny, I thought it was the other way around.'

'You know I'm interested in David and you're purposely trying to interfere,' Rebecca said angrily.

Maggie put a record on the stereo. 'You're interested in every man you meet. I can't see where David is any different from all the others. You'll tire of him in a week.'

'I won't. I've fallen in love with him.'

'Oh, Rebecca, what a silly thing you are. You only met the man a couple of

171

days ago, and now you're suddenly head over heels in love with him. You were also in love with my husband at one time, remember?' She hadn't intended mentioning Rod but it slipped out before she could check it.

'That isn't true,' Rebecca said, but she did not say it very convincingly.

'Of course it's true. Rod himself told me you told him you loved him.'

'He lied.'

'Rod never lied to me in his life. Even when I found you both in each other's arms he admitted that it hadn't been the first time. I understood him; I understand you.'

Rebecca looked suddenly contrite. 'Rod was different. I was unhappy with George. Rod made me laugh. But it was only a fleeting thing.'

'For you, perhaps. Although Rod came to me and cried on my shoulder, asking for my forgiveness which I gladly gave, I still think he loves you.'

'*Loves* me? Rod's dead. What difference does all that make now?'

'Is he dead, Rebecca?' Maggie asked.

172

'Of course he's dead. You know that.'

'I know nothing of the sort. They never found his body. When I see him buried in the ground I'll believe he's dead, but not until then.'

A Chopin nocturne played softly in the background.

'I love Rod very much,' Maggie said, letting herself drift into the familiar strains of the haunting melody. 'I'll forgive him anything just so long as he comes back to me. You'll not have him, Rebecca. I won't let you take him away from me.'

'He's dead, Maggie. Can't you understand that?'

'I don't believe it. I'm no fool, Rebecca. I know what you have up your sleeve but you'll not get away with it. I'm wise to you.'

Rebecca stared at her. 'What are you talking about? What do I have up my sleeve?'

Maggie bit her tongue and turned her back on her sister. 'There wasn't any earthquake last night, you know,' she said.

'How did you know that?'

'There wasn't, was there?'

'No. When we got into Pinebrook we met Mrs. Johnston and asked about the tremor. She said she didn't feel anything. Nobody at the café had felt it either.'

'There was an explosion in the cellar. That's why I was down there.'

'How did you know there was an explosion?'

'I smelled something I thought was gunpowder. I'm surprised that neither you nor David mentioned it. It came from the cellar. I went down to investigate.'

'And?'

'Someone had blown a small hole in one wall.' She described the condition in which she found the wall behind Heather Lambert's portrait. She didn't mention the portrait. Something told her not to.

'Why would anyone set off an explosion in the cellar?'

'Why would anyone want to kill poor Sophie?' Maggie let out a sigh. 'I don't know if it was dynamite . . . it wasn't that strong a blast. I thought at first it might have been . . . ' She was going to say, 'might have been Rod,' but instead, she

174

said, 'Oh, I don't know who it may have been. Someone from the village, perhaps, who'd hidden something there and didn't want us stumbling upon it.'

Rebecca looked frightened. 'I don't like it, Maggie. This whole bit is giving me the creeps. Ever since you set foot in this place weird things have been happening. And I for one don't plan on staying here very long. If you want to stay, then stay. I'm going. Where? I don't know. But I'm getting out of Heather House, as you call it, before it's too late.'

'Too late for what?'

'I don't know. I just feel that something terrible will happen if we stay here.'

'And where would you go?'

'I don't know that either.' Rebecca hesitated, as though choosing her words carefully and as though she wasn't sure she should say what she was tempted to say. 'I told David about how much I dislike living here. I thought maybe he could suggest something.'

'And what did David say?'

'He's on your side. He thinks I'm crazy to want to leave here.' She paused again.

'If you want to know the truth, he thinks you're the greatest since Cleopatra.'

Maggie was impressed but refused to let herself show it. 'Is that why he drove you home?'

'Don't be horrid.'

'He's a man, isn't he?' Maggie said. 'He's never married. He likes something new and different every so often. He's had you. Now he'll try to set his cap for me.'

'You're wrong. He doesn't think about you in that way at all. David is more innocent than you think.'

'Oh, sure . . . He's something right out of a Victorian melodrama, all virtuous and pure. I suppose it was his innocence that invited you into his bed? David McCloud is what was once called a cad. There's a slightly more distasteful word for his kind today.'

'Maggie, how rotten of you. David has said nothing but glowing things about you to me. He thinks most highly of you and you in turn talk about him like he was something that crawled out from the woodwork. How can you hate him and yet throw yourself at him the way you did?'

'I don't hate him. In fact, I don't think I'd actually mind getting to know him better. That way he could compare us and decide who is the better of the two. I think that's what's in his mind.'

'Maggie!' Rebecca's face was flushed. 'I can't believe my ears. This isn't you speaking. You're being monstrous.'

'No,' Maggie said casually, 'just truthful.'

'Well, don't you dare throw yourself at David. I won't permit it.'

Maggie grinned. 'Since when have you decided you can tell me what I can and cannot do? I'll do exactly as I please, sister dear . . . just as you have done all of your life.'

From out of nowhere came the scent of heather and in her mind Maggie saw Heather Lambert proud and defiant in her gilt frame. Maggie heard herself saying, 'Don't you dare interfere with me or you'll regret it,' in a voice that wasn't her own.

Rebecca took a step backward. 'Maggie,

what's gotten into you? You're behaving hatefully.'

'I'm behaving as I should have behaved years ago,' Maggie said. 'I've spoiled you rotten. I've always covered up for you. But no more, Rebecca. You can leave Heather House whenever you wish and you won't be missed . . . at least not by me.'

Rebecca stood there dumbstruck. She couldn't believe this was the same dear, loving sister she'd known all her life. The woman before her was a stranger. Even her voice was different. She saw the hatred in the eyes, the ugly down-curve of the mouth. 'Oh, Maggie, what's come over you? Something's happening to you and I don't know what it is.'

'I'm thinking of myself for a change. Is that so very wrong?'

'No, of course it isn't wrong, but don't look at me like that. You look as though you hate me.'

Maggie suddenly slumped back against the stereo. 'I'm tired, Rebecca. Go to bed.'

Her sister came over to her and put her arm around Maggie's shoulder. 'No wonder. Finding Sophie . . . '

'Please, Rebecca, let's not talk anymore. I'm very tired.'

'Of course you're tired, Maggie. You've
been rummaging round the house and in
the cellar ever since you got back, besides
your being so distraught about what
happened to Sophie.'

Maggie patted her hand. She could
only vaguely remember the things that
had been said. It was like a receding echo
far back in the inner recesses of her mind.
Despite her cat nap that afternoon, she
felt so very drowsy again. She needed to
sleep. The day was a blur in her memory.
Rebecca's face was a blur. For a moment
she was sure it was some other woman's
face, a woman who was a stranger to her
and yet not a stranger.

'Edwina,' Maggie said softly.

Rebecca cocked her head. 'Edwina?
Who's Edwina?'

Maggie shook herself. 'What? What did
I say?'

'You said, 'Edwina.' '

'Did I? I wonder why.'

'Come on,' Rebecca said, 'you're

exhausted, let's go to bed.' She reached behind Maggie and switched off the music.

'No, you go along. I'll be all right.' She moved, as though through a vacuum, toward the foyer and the stairs that would take her to her bedroom. She wanted to be alone with her thoughts.

As she entered the bedroom, she thought she caught a glimpse of white chiffon with a blur of purple heather drifting swiftly across the room. It seemed to stand poised for a second against the white sheet that covered the broken window.

Heather . . . Heather Lambert.

10

Maggie sat on the edge of the bed, staring at the sheet that covered the broken window. She saw nothing, heard nothing but the dull throbbing of her heart. A strange swirling noise rushed around inside her head and a dizziness came over her.

The air in the room was suddenly stifling. She was suffocating. She felt a desperate need for air. The room was still pungent with the odor of burned cloth from the night before.

The reminder of the fire brought her to her feet. She made her way slowly toward one of the unbroken windows and tried to raise it. It refused to budge. The others, too, refused to surrender to her efforts to open them.

She went toward the sheet-draped window and ripped the covering away. Strangely enough the air in the room refused to freshen. Nothing seemed to pass into the room from the night outside. It was as if an invisible barrier had been built, holding out the night.

Something white again moved across her field of vision. The door to the hall was standing open. Now it began to move, threatening to slam shut. Maggie made a dash for it, flinging it back. It banged noisily against the wall, its knob leaving a dent into the plaster.

She mustn't let the door close.

Frantically she looked about the room for something with which to prop it open and spied a small chest of drawers. She put her back against the chest and strained and pushed, sliding it across the rug.

'Maggie, what on earth?'

Rebecca was standing in the doorway. The room was as it should be. The air was fresh and clean and cold as it poured through the broken window. Maggie sucked in great quantities of it, filling her lungs, letting it settle her head.

'What are you doing?' Rebecca glanced at the pulled-down sheet. 'Why did you rip the sheet off the window?'

'I couldn't breathe. The room was stifling,' Maggie gasped. 'And the door . . . it slammed shut last night and stuck. I couldn't open it. There must be a draft. It almost blew closed again. I was wedging it open.'

'Of course there's a draft, that window's broken out. Maggie, this room is freezing. Why don't you come down and sleep with me?'

'No,' Maggie said. 'I'm sleeping here. I'll be all right now, Rebecca. Go to bed.'

'No, I insist. You'll just catch cold sleeping here. Come along. We'll sleep in my bed. It'll be like old times. I'll make us some hot chocolate and we can talk . . . just like we used to.'

'No, Rebecca. Really, I'll be all right now. I'm tired. I don't want to talk. I just want to sleep.'

'So we won't talk then. Please, Maggie. Do it for my sake. Sleep with me. This house makes me nervous. I feel so alone down there.'

Rebecca came over to her and put her arms around her. 'Don't be angry with me, Maggie. I know I'm nothing but a silly child at times. Don't lecture me . . . not anymore tonight. We've both had a difficult time of it these past few days and it would be nice just to forget all that's happened and everything that's been said and start all over again tomorrow after a good night's sleep.'

Maggie dropped onto the edge of the bed, saying nothing.

'Oh, Maggie. Please don't make me sleep in this drafty, cold room. I will if you don't agree to come down and sleep in my room. I just don't want to be alone.'

Maggie didn't want her here in this room that had once been Heather Lambert's. She didn't want anyone sleeping in Heather's bed but herself . . . and Rod, in time.

Perhaps Rebecca was right. The room was too cold. She might catch a cold. She was always catching a cold. Slowly she got to her feet. 'I'll sleep in your room,' she said resignedly. 'Go along. I'll change and be down in a moment.'

Rebecca gave her a squeeze. 'Thank you, Maggie. You really are good to me.'

What had happened to her resolution not to give in to Rebecca ever again? Maggie asked herself as she took off the lovely burgundy dress and tossed it over the back of a chair. She remembered a passage she'd once read, though she couldn't remember the author:

There is no such thing in man's nature as a settled and full resolve either for good or evil, except at the very moment of execution.

My moment of execution is not yet at hand, Maggie reminded herself. She did not rightly understand what was going on in this house. Something was affecting her from time to time, pulling her first in one direction and then in the other, as if opposing forces were fighting over the right to control her.

She had scoffed at David's mention of ghosts. Now she was not so eager or so ready to scoff. She felt sure that the ghost of Heather Lambert was trying to influence her, and maybe someone else as well. There was definitely something here. She was certain of that. If it wasn't a ghost, it was some other spirit, some force, some power or some person controlling her . . . or trying to.

Was it this strange spirit, this force; this white, filmy, ghostly figure that had set fire to this room? Was it Heather Lambert who wanted to see her destroyed?

She met Rebecca at the foot of the steps. Rebecca had two mugs of hot chocolate and some cookies on a tray.

'I thought these might help you sleep,' Rebecca said.

'I don't need anything to help me sleep. I'm almost asleep on my feet as it is.'

'Nevertheless, a little more inducement can't hurt. It'll relax you all the more.'

Rebecca's room was stark and narrow and austere. Why she wanted to sleep in it Maggie couldn't imagine, but after looking closely at it she reckoned that her original suspicions were correct. There were French doors leading out onto a terrace that overlooked the patio and the driveway. It would be a simple matter for someone to come and go without anyone else in the house knowing of it.

'I was thinking about what you found in the basement,' Rebecca said as she propped herself up on pillows and tossed a cookie into her mouth. 'What do you think is down there?'

'I'm too tired to think about it tonight, Rebecca. Go to sleep.'

'Drink your hot chocolate before it cools off. I put a marshmallow in it, the way you like it.'

With a sigh Maggie reached for the cup of hot chocolate. It was thick and sweet. She took a deep swallow.

'Maybe this place was used for some kind of smuggling,' Rebecca suggested.

'Smuggling?' Maggie asked sleepily.

'Sure. David said the house has been vacant for a terribly long time. Everyone suspects it's haunted so nobody comes near here. It would make a perfect spot to hide smuggled goods . . . or maybe a body.'

'You're being overly dramatic. Go to sleep.'

'Maybe old man Lambert is buried down there.'

'Louis Lambert went away.'

'Yes, but nobody saw him go, David says. Maybe this Heather Lambert lady knocked him over the head and she and Sophie carried him down to the cellar.'

'Oh, really, Rebecca.'

'It's possible, you know . . . Maybe someone got rid of Sophie for fear she might spill the beans.'

'But hardly likely. Heather Lambert was supposed to have died of a broken heart. If she killed her husband she wouldn't continue to pine for him, now, would she?'

'Then maybe it wasn't Mr. Lambert who Heather and Sophie killed. Maybe Mr. Lambert killed one of Heather's admirers and ran off.'

'Why would he run off without Heather if he loved her enough to kill for her?' Maggie finished the hot chocolate and fluffed up her pillow. 'Go to sleep. I don't want to think about all this anymore.'

'How did you know Heather Lambert died of a broken heart?'

'The workman who came to fix the window and paint the door was talking about it. Turn off the light, Rebecca.'

'Why did you have him paint the door white?'

Maggie yawned. 'He said the people around here would look more neighborly on us if we had a white door. Rather than argue I told him to go ahead and paint it.'

'David told me all kinds of things about this house. Do you want to hear them?'

Maggie didn't answer. She kept her breathing even and feigned sleep, which she knew she wouldn't have to fake for very long, despite Rebecca's chatter and the horrors of the night. She suddenly felt very peaceful.

'Mrs. Johnston used to live here. Did you know that?' Rebecca asked. 'She moved out when she married that man who's now in the wheelchair. Some people say old man Lambert frightened her away by trying to make passes at her.' Rebecca giggled. 'Who would ever think old Mrs. Johnston was ever pretty enough to attract a man? But David said she wasn't all that bad when she was young. Right after she got married — or was it just before she got married? — Mr. Lambert ran off with a young girl from Pinebrook. The townspeople were furious. He had a reputation for seducing

189

young things. He must have been some hunk of man. They say Heather Lambert was jealous as the dickens of him.' She glanced over at Maggie and saw her regular breathing. 'Are you asleep, Maggie?'

Maggie stayed silent.

Rebecca sighed her disappointment. 'Suit yourself. Don't say I didn't try to tell you.' She clicked off the lamp beside the bed.

Tell me what? Maggie wondered, but she was too tired to ask.

11

She overslept.

Rebecca was gone when Maggie awoke. The day was overcast but Maggie's mood, in spite of Sophie's murder, was unusually bright. She was glad when she found Rebecca's note saying she'd gone off with David McCloud. They'd gone for a drive.

Maggie didn't want Rebecca underfoot. There was so much to be done. She would get Heather Lambert's portrait back where it belonged and give all the rooms a good cleaning, not only the surface cleaning that poor Sophie had done. There was painting to be done, rugs to be taken up, and the furniture in the living room had to be moved around. She didn't quite understand why she had to rearrange the furniture, but she had to.

She worked hard, refusing to let herself think about Sophie and her murderer. After all, the girl was virtually a stranger, so why should her death affect her? But it wasn't Sophie's death that bothered her so much as it was the act of murder. As for the murderer, Maggie didn't feel afraid of him; she felt sure she knew his identity although she hoped she was wrong.

The portrait in the cellar posed a problem until the carpenter showed up to work on the window in Maggie's bedroom.

'Mr. Babcock,' Maggie called as the man started up the stairs with his box of tools, 'could you please help me carry something up from the cellar? I'm afraid it's too large and cumbersome for me to manage alone.'

'Be glad to, Mrs. Garrison.' He put down his tools and followed her into the kitchen. 'Too bad about poor old Sophie. Terrible, the things that happen these days. Some old tramp, they say it was.'

Maggie merely nodded, not wanting to encourage conversation along that line. 'I'm afraid the light is burned out down there so we'll have to use this old kerosene lamp.'

He took it from her, lit it and they went down the dark wooden steps slowly.

'Yep, can't tell who's running around the streets these days. Now, me ... I don't trust nobody,' he said.

At the bottom of the steps Maggie said, 'Over there against that far wall, there's a portrait of Heather Lambert which I really don't think should be left down here to decay. It belongs up in the living room.'

'Oh, yes indeed,' Mr. Babcock said as he reached the other side of the cellar and stood looking up at Heather Lambert. He held the lantern high, bringing the face to life. 'That's old Heather, all right. Wonder who dragged the old girl down here?'

'It's such a lovely painting,' Maggie said. 'It's a pity to hide it away like this.'

Together they moved the painting away from the wall. When they did Maggie noticed the bricks — a few of which had been blown away near the floor — were covering a doorway. She rested her edge of the portrait down on the ground again and looked at the bricked-up doorway.

'I wonder what's behind there,' she said.

'Old cesspool,' Mr. Babcock said. 'Remember Miss Heather complaining about it. Was always overflowing and smelling up the place. She had a septic tank put in outside. Must have had somebody come in and brick up the old room where the cesspool was.'

'Did you brick it up, Mr. Babcock?'

'Nope. Don't know who did that. It's none of my handiwork.'

Maggie didn't give the bricked-up room any more thought. A foul-smelling cesspool held no interest for her, although it was obviously of interest to someone. It was possible, of course, that someone wanted to get them out of Heather House and decided to knock over the bricks, hoping the repugnant smells would rout them. Every town had its mischief-makers and its busybodies.

Between them they carried Heather Lambert back into the living room, hanging her across from Louis Lambert, where she rightfully belonged.

'Certainly was a handsome woman, Mrs. Garrison,' the carpenter said as he stood looking up at Heather.

'Did you know her, Mr. Babcock?'

'Not socially, of course. Used to do a few odd things about here for her and him.'

'Did you like them?'

He looked at her with a strange expression on his face. 'Like them? How do you mean?'

'Were they nice to work for? Did they treat everyone well?'

'Okay, I guess. She was a nice lady. Him, he wasn't nothing much. A real snob. Not regular like you folks. Thought he owned everybody. Him and Miss Heather were as different as day and night.' He scratched his head. 'Nobody could figure out why poor Miss Heather could have been so blind to his ways.'

'What ways?'

Mr. Babcock lowered his head but raised his eyes. 'Had the morals of an alley cat. Right under her nose, too. Everybody used to try to warn Miss Heather about him but she only got mad at them and flew off the handle. Told them all to mind their own business and she'd take care of hers.' He gave a soft little chuckle. 'A real little wildcat, that Miss Heather, but when it came to him, she never raised her voice. Loved him more than life, everybody says.'

'I understand she just died without any reason,' Maggie said.

'Yep. A broken heart, the old doc said. Just sat up in that tower window all day and all night watching and waiting and hoping for that no-good husband of hers to come back.' He shook his head slowly from side to side. 'A pity. A real pity, if you ask me.'

'A woman's love is very different from that of a man's, Mr. Babcock. We feel differently about things. And when we love a man, we can overlook and forgive just about anything in the world, just so long as we won't lose him.'

Mr. Babcock scratched the back of his head. 'Never could understand you ladyfolk. That's why I stayed a bachelor all these years. I tried once. Never could make hide nor hair out of that girl, so I just left her and all the rest of them alone.'

Maggie laughed softly. 'You just didn't

try hard enough. Well, I'm keeping you from your work. Do you think you'll have that window upstairs finished today?'

'Nope. Had to order the panes from over in Anderson. They won't be here for a day or two.'

'I see.' She hesitated. 'By the way, Mr. Babcock, I'll need some men to move furniture for me, take up some of the rugs, things like that. Would you know anyone to recommend?'

'Could do it myself, with Charlie Pickendaw's help.'

'Good. Do you think he'd be available tomorrow?'

'Old Charlie's available all the time. Don't work at all. Never did. Just plain lazy, I guess.'

'Would you bring him tomorrow . . . early?'

'Be glad to, Mrs. Garrison.' He cocked his head. 'Pay in cash, though. Old Charlie don't like checks and banks much. Likes to collect his pay by the day. Only works day to day when he works, which ain't often.'

'I'll stop at the bank and have cash on

hand,' Maggie said.

Mr. Babcock scratched his head again. 'Of course, if you're going into town you might ask him yourself. Old Charlie's a funny cuss. Don't like to work for nobody he ain't met before. Stays in a room at old Mrs. Johnston's. Ain't much of a room, but it's a room and Mrs. Johnston lets him work off the rent and meals by doing odd jobs around the place for her. Husband ain't worth nothing; just sits around in that wheelchair of his sleeping and staring into space, never talking to nobody, never doing anything but sitting and staring.'

Maggie didn't relish the idea of going to Mrs. Johnston's, but the work needed to be done and old Charlie Pickendaw was a chance at getting it done. 'I'll stop and talk with him,' she said.

* * *

Maggie knew the town would be buzzing with talk of Sophie's murder, but she girded herself for it. She decided she would not speak of it to anyone.

198

At the hardware store she bought the largest flashlight they had, together with several dozen light bulbs of different sizes. She picked out paint for the breakfast room and told them to hold it, that Mr. Babcock would pick it up.

She finished her other chores . . . buying more Chopin recordings, a stack of change-of-address cards from the post office and a supply of writing paper from the stationery store. She stopped at the library and got a library card. She checked at the freight office about her trunks, knowing, however, that they couldn't possibly have arrived yet.

Every stop she made she could tell people were anxious to talk about Sophie's death, but Maggie held herself as aloof as possible and did not encourage any conversation that started to lean in the direction of the horrible happenings of the previous evening.

She was tempted to stop at David McCloud's office and check on his and Rebecca's whereabouts. She did not.

At the Johnston house, Mr. Johnston was sitting in his wheelchair sunning himself on the porch, although there wasn't much sun. The gray still lingered heavy in the sky, casting a pall over everything except Maggie's spirits.

'Good day,' she said cheerfully. 'You must be Mr. Johnston. I'm Maggie Garrison. I was looking for a Mr. Pickendaw.'

Mr. Johnston kept his eyes fixed on Maggie's face. He didn't speak for a moment. He just kept looking at her. Then he said, 'You're the one who's living in the Lambert place?' His voice was low and smooth.

'Yes, my sister and I leased it just the other day.'

'I see.' He breathed a deep sigh. 'I suppose it was inevitable.'

'I beg your pardon?' Maggie frowned.

He shook his head. 'Never mind. I think aloud sometimes. Bad habit of mine.' He turned his chair and wheeled it toward the front door of the house. 'Charlie's inside somewhere. Come on, I'll show you his room.' He pushed himself forward. Maggie opened the door for him.

'I'm sorry to trouble you. Isn't Mrs.

Johnston at home?'

He didn't answer. He propelled himself down the hallway toward the back of the house. 'Charlie,' he called in a loud, angry voice, 'somebody to see you.' When no one answered the man yelled, 'Charlie, blast it, where the devil are you?' Still no answer. 'Must be out back,' he said, scowling.

'Please,' Maggie said. 'I am being a bother to you. I can come back another time.'

'You're a bother all right,' Mr. Johnston said, glowering at her. 'Why don't you two women go back where you came from? You're not wanted here, you know.'

'Sir,' Maggie said sharply, 'I am sorry if I've troubled you. You can be sure I will not do so again.'

She let the door bang shut after her and didn't realize that she was shaking with rage until she got outside. The nerve of him, she thought as she walked hurriedly toward her car.

'You looking for me, lady?' someone called.

She turned and saw a heavy-set man

201

coming out of the house and hurrying down the steps.

'I'm Charlie Pickendaw.'

'Yes,' she said curtly, managing a smile although she was still angry. 'I'm Maggie Garrison. Mr. Babcock said you might be interested in helping him do some work around my house. I'm the new tenant of Heather Lambert's place.'

'The Lambert place, huh?'

'Yes,' she said in a sharp-edged voice.

'What kind of work?' He squinted, studying her face.

She told him.

'Well, don't know.' He stroked his chin with his forefinger and thumb.

'I haven't all day to waste, Mr. Pickendaw. If you're not interested I am sure I will find someone who is.'

To her surprise the man laughed. 'Doubt it, Mrs. Garrison. There ain't many who'd work there, exceptin' maybe Babcock and me.'

'And why not, may I ask?'

'After what happened to old Sophie . . . and then there's Heather Lambert's ghost, of course. Don't believe in ghosts

202

myself. Me and old Babcock don't believe in much exceptin' ourselves maybe.'

'There are no ghosts in Heather House,' Maggie said angrily. She thought briefly of that white, wispy thing that had hovered in her bedroom the night before but pushed it off with a shake of her head. 'I do not intend standing here all day arguing that point. Do you want to work for me or don't you?'

'Feisty! Just like her. Look a little like her, too.' The man laughed again. 'Sure, okay, Mrs. Garrison. I'll come. When do you want me?'

'Mr. Babcock said he'd pick you up in the morning if that's all right with you. Early.'

'Tomorrow, then. Early. Pay in cash. No checks. Don't like banks and don't like nothin' I can't spend at the roadhouse.'

'Cash is fine. I'll see you in the morning, then. Good day, Mr. Pickendaw.'

Mr. Pickendaw was still laughing low in his throat as she got back into the Mercedes. She'd forgotten about the bank and was doubly annoyed when the clock on the dashboard reminded her it was a quarter of three. But was that really why she was annoyed? Or was it the continual mention of ghosts . . . and a ghost she'd possibly seen herself? Or maybe the rudeness of Mr. Johnston?

She gave an angry grunt as she switched on the ignition. The Johnstons . . . they deserved each other, she thought. Well, she wouldn't have anything to do with them in the future.

It was late. She'd have to hurry if she intended to reach the bank before three o'clock.

As she drove off she happened to glance in the rear-view mirror. Mrs. Johnston had come out onto the porch and was standing there, arms folded tightly across her chest. Maggie could almost feel the cold, hateful stare stabbing into her back.

★　★　★

Rebecca had not returned home.

Maggie started to worry as she fixed dinner. There was no one to call to inquire about Rebecca except David, and there was no answer when she dialed his number. She could, of course, drive into Pinebrook, but she might pass Rebecca on the drive there, not being able to see her in the dark. Besides, where in Pinebrook would she search other than David's apartment? Anyway, she refused to face the Johnstons again.

She went to Heather's portrait and looked into the painted eyes. 'He'll come back to me,' she said. 'I'm sure of it.'

But the minute she looked away from Heather her strength seemed to go out of her. Perhaps Rebecca wasn't with David. Perhaps she was with Rod, wherever he was hiding. Perhaps they were plotting to try again at getting her out of the way.

Maggie served herself dinner and sat at the table in the kitchen to eat.

What about George? she wondered. Did they kill Rebecca's husband to keep him quiet? It was unlikely that George would benefit from all this. Rebecca didn't want him, although it seemed unlikely that Rod would be capable of murdering his best friend. Rebecca, however, never stopped at anything until she got what she was after, even if she did not want it after she got it. She had a way of making people — men in particular — do just about anything she asked.

Murder? Yes, even that, Maggie had to admit. She shuddered, recalling those terrible old memories.

12

Rebecca still had not returned by morning.

Despite a somewhat sleepless night, Maggie woke in the morning anxious to get to the work that needed to be done around the house. The sound of a car driving up brought Maggie to her feet. She hurried to the front door, but it wasn't Rebecca, it was the carpenter and Charlie Peckindaw.

After she set the men to work she picked up the telephone and dialed David McCloud's office number. 'This is Mrs. Garrison,' she said to the young lady who answered.

'Oh, hi, Mrs. Garrison. Everything all right?'

'Yes, thank you. Is Mr. McCloud in?'

'No. He took some people out to see a piece of property.'

'Did he say how long he'd be gone?'

'Maybe an hour or so,' the girl said.

'Can I help with anything?'

'No, thank you. Just have him call me.' She hesitated. She was tempted to ask the girl if Rebecca had been with David, but she decided it was best not to stir up possible gossip. 'Thank you,' she said abruptly and hung up.

'Where do you want this old chest?' Mr. Babcock asked as he and Charlie Pickendaw picked up a walnut *mudejar* chest with ivory inlay.

'Under that window,' Maggie said, pointing. Watching the men move it across the room, she wondered why she instinctively knew that was the right place for the piece. 'I'd like the piano turned the other way around and that refectory table placed up against that wall,' she told them.

About three o'clock Mr. Babcock and Charlie Pickendaw said they were ready to quit for the day. Maggie paid Charlie and told Mr. Babcock she'd see him tomorrow. She reminded him about the paint she'd bought at the hardware store. He said he'd pick it up.

Just as they drove off Maggie heard

another car and turned to see David's sedan come up the driveway. 'Hi,' David said, getting out of the car with a wave of his hand. 'I wanted to return your call but I was coming out this way anyway, so I decided I'd stop.'

'Isn't Rebecca with you?' she asked, looking toward the car.

'That's what I wanted to talk to you about.' He took her arm and ushered her back inside the house.

'Is anything the matter?' she asked anxiously as they went into the living room.

'Hey,' he said, noticing the new arrangement of the furniture. 'It looks great.' His eyes went to the portrait of Heather Lambert. 'Where on earth did you find that?'

'In the cellar,' Maggie said hastily. 'Where's Rebecca? What's wrong, David?'

David continued to look up at the portrait. 'You know,' he said glancing at Maggie, 'there's a great resemblance between you and Mrs. Lambert.'

'Oh, never mind the portrait, David. What is the matter?'

'Nothing's the matter,' he said. There

was a hesitancy in his voice. 'At least I don't think so.' He took her arm and seated her on the divan before the fireplace. He glanced toward the liquor cabinet that had been moved to the opposite side of the room. 'Do you mind if I have a drink?'

'No, of course not. Help yourself.' She watched him anxiously as he poured a double shot of Scotch into a glass and downed it. 'Something is wrong. Where's Rebecca?' Her hands tightened in her lap.

'Oh, don't worry. Rebecca's fine . . . just fine.' He poured himself another drink and carried it back to the couch and sat down beside Maggie, rolling the glass back and forth between his hands. 'I know you must have been worried sick with Rebecca being away all day and night.'

'It isn't the first time,' Maggie said. She tried to sound calm and unconcerned, but inside her stomach was fluttering.

'Well, Rebecca wanted to drive into San Francisco yesterday morning.'

Maggie's heart stopped . . . or seemed to.

David gave a boyish smile. 'You know your sister; she's hard to say no to.'

Maggie gave a quick nod and leaned toward him, silently coaxing him to go on, but she was thinking: it had all started in San Francisco once before.

'Well, you know it isn't much of a drive, really, and we had a good enough time.'

'Is she still there?'

'No, she's up at my place.' He looked at her. 'I think I told you I have a little weekend cabin up in the mountains.'

Maggie breathed a sigh of relief.

David hesitated. He rolled the glass between his hands for a second or two, then put it to his lips and emptied it. 'She wasn't feeling too hot so I told her to . . .'

'Not feeling well? Is she sick?' She touched his arm.

'Not sick, exactly.' He gave her a look that needed no further explanation.

Maggie felt her face flush. 'I see,' she said, looking down at her lap.

'I had some clients I had to see this morning, so I couldn't stay with her.'

'I understand.'

David fumbled with the empty glass again. 'Mind if I help myself to another? I've had quite a day.'

Maggie shook her head impatiently.

David got up and went over to the cabinet and splashed more Scotch into his glass. 'Rebecca's quite a girl,' he said. He gave another nervous little laugh. 'She has a way about her that makes me feel like a high-school kid again.'

Maggie sighed. 'Yes, Rebecca's like that.'

'We did some pretty crazy things . . . things I never thought I'd ever do.'

Maggie straightened her back and gave him a suspicious look. 'Why are you telling me all this, David? I am very well acquainted with my sister. I know her behavior almost as well as I know my own. She has always been a rather rash and reckless young lady. I have never tried to interfere; I don't wish to do so now.' She noticed that her hands were trembling ever so slightly.

'It's crazy,' David said, draining the glass. 'When I'm alone with her I do things I feel I might regret later.'

'Then you should stay away from her if you believe her to be a bad influence. But really, David, you are a grown man, a man with a good business mind; and having known you only a day or two I would say you were quite capable of being your own master. Rebecca is not some siren trying to lure you onto the rocks.'

'Oh, please, Maggie. Don't get me wrong. I'm not putting Rebecca down. On the contrary. I think I'm in love with her.'

Maggie glanced up at Heather Lambert's portrait. Rebecca hadn't disappointed her, she thought. And she'd acted fast . . . faster than Maggie had expected.

David cleared his throat. He started to get up for another drink but changed his mind and set the glass aside. 'I'm aware that I don't know very much about Rebecca, but I hinted about our getting married last night.'

Maggie smiled to herself, knowing Heather Lambert was smiling, too.

'And what did Rebecca say?'

'Oh, I didn't come right out and

propose.' He shook his head. 'I never thought I'd even want to propose to any girl. But somehow Rebecca got to me.' He looked at Maggie. 'I thought I had better talk to you first.'

Maggie gave him a frosty look. 'Are you here to ask my consent?'

David looked shocked. 'No, not at all. To be perfectly blunt, I'm here to try to decide which of you I am more attracted to.'

Maggie glowered at him. 'You are rather loose with your attentions. Do they always stray so easily?' He reached for her hand but she withdrew it and stood up. She wandered over to the window and stood there looking out.

'Only when two such beautiful women as you come into my life.' He said it easily.

Maggie walked over to the fireplace and leaned on the mantel. 'If you are here to make love to me so that you might compare me with Rebecca, I suggest you leave. You are a very likable man, David, but you are behaving in quite an unbecoming manner.'

David shook his head and cursed silently to himself. 'I don't understand myself. I swear Rebecca's put a spell of some kind on me.'

'I can assure you,' Maggie said haughtily, 'my sister is no witch.'

Again David shook his head. 'I'm not so sure about that.'

'You'd be doing me a service, David, if you would drive Rebecca home this evening . . . that is, if she wishes to come.'

David studied her for a moment. 'You're as cold as Rebecca says you are, Maggie.'

'I suppose I am,' she admitted.

David studied her for a moment, then turned and walked across the room. He mounted the two steps to the foyer. He turned around and started to say something.

'Please, David,' Maggie cut off whatever he'd been about to say. 'Some other time.'

He shrugged his shoulders, turned and walked out of the house. Maggie waited until the door closed before she let the air out of her lungs.

'So Rebecca is up to her old tricks

again,' she said aloud. She supposed she should warn David but, like Rod, he wouldn't listen. Why were all men so blind to Rebecca's wiles? But if Rebecca was with David, then she might forget completely about Rod . . . at least for the time being.

Rod would come looking for her, Maggie told herself. She stood up suddenly. Yes, Rod would come; she was convinced of it, and when he did . . .

She smiled. Her plans were working out after all.

13

The night shadows were comforting after a bustling, busy day. Maggie was curled up in her favorite spot, on the couch in front of the fireplace of the newly arranged living room; a spot where she had but to glance up to see Heather Lambert keeping her company.

Her favorite Chopin music was playing softly. A book of poetry lay open in her lap but her eyes were raised from the page, staring at the flickering flames in the fireplace.

If Rebecca would only go away and leave her in peace, leave her to wait for Rod to come home. He was near; she could feel it. She wanted him so very much.

She knew, however, that she'd never be able to hold Rod for very long with Rebecca constantly on the scene. He'd never listen if she tried to tell him — as she'd done many times before — that Rebecca was not the kind of woman he would be happy with for the rest of his life.

There was little doubt in her mind now that Rebecca had started the fire. She doubted, too, that David knew of it. Rebecca had moved the candles while David was somewhere else in the house. He was as innocent as Rod, if blind love could be called innocent. Rebecca was a superb actress and a great manipulator when it came to getting her own way.

Maggie remembered the so-called hysterics over George's death, hysterics Rebecca put on for the benefit of friends. She wallowed in their sympathy. Her hysteria, however, was only an excuse to indulge herself in an unnatural wildness. She had resorted to excesses that made her friends gasp. But poor Rebecca was in deep, deep mourning, they told themselves, and they averted their eyes from her dreadful behavior and tried to overlook it. As time passed, however, Rebecca had forgotten she was supposed to be grieving and the gossip about her began to circulate.

The headlights of a car flashed across

the windows. Maggie straightened up, listening as a car door opened and slammed shut. She heard Rebecca call good night and then the car drove off. A moment later Rebecca walked into the living room.

'Well, I see you decided to come home,' Maggie said.

Rebecca didn't answer. She went to the liquor cabinet and fixed herself a drink. 'Want one?'

Maggie shook her head impatiently.

Rebecca tilted the glass and downed the liquor. 'Ah, I needed that,' she said. She started across the room in the direction of her bedroom.

'I don't suppose you intend telling me where you have been,' Maggie said.

'Sure. I didn't think you were interested.' Rebecca dropped into a chair and looked around the room. 'You've changed everything around, I see.'

'Don't change the subject. Where were you, Rebecca?'

'With David, of course. We went up to his cabin in the mountains.'

'You also went to San Francisco, I understand.'

Rebecca glanced at her. Her eyes narrowed. 'How did you know that?'

'David told me.'

'David? When did you speak with him?'

'This afternoon. He came to see me, thinking I might be worried about you.'

Rebecca looked angry. 'He never mentioned it.'

'You are obviously intent upon destroying yourself again, Rebecca. Well, go ahead, but kindly do not do it here. What you do outside this house is of no concern to me; however, what you do inside Heather House is very much my concern.'

To her surprise Rebecca laughed. 'You and your precious house and your antiquated morals.' She stood up and stretched. 'Just don't get too comfortable in this house, Maggie, my love. You won't be here very long.'

'And what, may I ask, does that mean?'

Rebecca gave her a wide, innocent smile. 'Didn't David tell you? Isn't that why he really stopped here this afternoon?'

'Tell me what?' She felt a strange tightening in the pit of her stomach.

'This old relic,' Rebecca said, waving her arms, 'is going to be pulled down around your delicate ears.'

'What?'

Rebecca continued to look smug. 'Yes. Those men David had to see this morning were from the state highway department. They're buying up land for the construction of a freeway. Good old Heather House is smack in the middle of its path.'

'But I intend buying it. I'll never sell.'

'It isn't for sale anymore. The town Council has already given it over to the state. You'll be hearing from them soon, advising you of the change of ownership. Oh, they aren't going to raze it immediately. Maybe in a couple of months . . . a year even.'

Maggie was horror-stricken. 'But they can't do that. This house isn't Pinebrook's property to sell. It belongs to the Lamberts.'

Rebecca shrugged. 'Something about eminent domain or something like that. David knew about it all the time but he was anxious for the commission the town paid him when he leased it. He got his commission check yesterday and today he brought in the men from the state.'

'I don't believe you.'

'Well, believe it or not, it is the truth.'

Maggie took a deep breath and stiffened her back. 'I won't permit it. They won't get away with it. This is *my* house.'

'Your house? Are you mad? You're just a tenant.'

'I have a lease.'

'We have a lease, remember? The state can buy back the lease and I as joint tenant can sell it to them.'

'Over my dead body!'

Rebecca merely shrugged her shoulders. 'Have it your own way,' she said and turned and walked out of the room.

14

As she dressed the next morning, Maggie went over the plan she had formulated.

First she would have to manipulate Rebecca into running off with David . . . for good. Then she'd wait until Rod showed up looking for Rebecca. She had no fear for her life insofar as Rod was concerned. She could manage him easily enough. Rebecca wouldn't make any more attempts on Maggie's life now that she had David. Of course, if Rebecca decided she needed Maggie's insurance money, her life was still in danger. So she would have to get Rebecca away, and immediately. She knew exactly how she would handle Rebecca.

Rebecca was sitting out on the patio sipping coffee when Maggie came downstairs. Her sister looked up over the rim of her cup. She smiled. 'Good grief, Maggie, you look worse than I feel.'

'I didn't sleep too well,' Maggie said.

'Here, this might help,' Rebecca said as she poured her sister a cup of coffee and handed it across the table. 'It's doing wonders for me.'

Maggie rubbed the back of her neck. 'You could have let me know you would be gone overnight.'

'I didn't expect to be gone that long.'

Maggie scowled at Rebecca. 'I suppose you are up to your old tricks again.'

'What old tricks?' Rebecca looked at her with wide, innocent eyes.

'If you are,' Maggie said, ignoring Rebecca's question, 'I wholeheartedly suggest you leave David McCloud out of them. I don't think he felt too comfortable with your little tour of San Francisco.'

'What are you trying to say?'

'David told me he was a little concerned about you. He thinks he'd prefer a woman with a little more maturity . . . like me. He told me as much when he stopped by yesterday.'

'You keep your hands off David,' Rebecca said in an angry whisper.

Maggie merely grinned. 'You have it wrong, dear. It seems to be the other way around. You'd better tell David to keep his hands off *me*, if you're interested in him.'

'David doesn't want you. You're too old for him.'

'All men have a mother complex, didn't you know that?'

'I'm warning you, Maggie. Lay off.'

'That I can't promise. David is a very handsome man. I know he's interested in me and I might just see if I can get him.'

'I'll not tell you again, Maggie. David is *mine*.'

'Then I suggest you better tell him not to come to the house anymore. I might find I couldn't trust myself,' she said glibly as she sipped her coffee. 'Remember how you dallied with Rod. He wound up falling in love with me simply because you couldn't make up your mind.'

They heard a car pull into the driveway and honk its horn.

'Is that David?' Maggie asked, getting out of her chair. 'I'll go let him in.'

'No.' Rebecca flung back her chair and almost ran from the house.

Maggie merely smiled and settled

herself in the chair, sipping her coffee. Poor, predictable Rebecca. It was so easy to manage her.

When she heard the car drive off, Maggie got out of her chair and went up the stairs, toward the room at the top of the tower. She seated herself at the window. She'd wait for Rod.

15

The wind had come up strong and blustery, bending trees, pelting the house from all sides with dust and leaves and loosened debris; a strange, almost unearthly gale that seemed to blow from all four directions at once. It moaned low in its throat, like a threatening beast. Maggie could feel the force of it trying to get in at her. The walls fought back against the lashing winds, holding her safe inside her refuge.

She sat, curled up on the divan before the fire, looking down at the book she held in her hand. She'd found it on a table in the tower room. It was large and squarish and heavy, bound in dark Moroccan leather with gold tooling. There was no printing on the cover or spine, just an initial 'H.'

She flipped open the pages. They were covered with the graceful scrawl of a woman's handwriting.

'Louis left today,' she read. 'I'm not going to let myself be too unduly concerned. He loves me, I'm sure. He will be back. I will sit and wait for him if it takes forever.'

Maggie flipped to the fly leaf. 'HEATHER LAMBERT' was written there. She went to the last entry in the diary.

'Edwina is to be married. I'm glad she will be living here no longer. Now I can wait in peace for Louis to come back to me.'

How so like herself, Maggie thought as she put the book aside. Here she sat waiting for a husband who had disappeared, presumably dead, although she knew differently. She had gotten Rebecca out of the house and, like Heather Lambert, could now wait in peace for Rod to come back. Maggie got up and switched the stereo on. The familiar strains of the Chopin nocturne drifted through the room. She settled herself on the couch again, intending to let herself melt into the music, but her mind wandered . . .

She remembered when she was only nine years old and her father and mother doted on her. She had been their favorite then because they had no other children. She almost wished now that she was that little girl again; she wanted to be loved and pampered and cherished.

When Rebecca was born, everything changed. Maggie was made to share and Rebecca broke the windows of the playhouse and pulled the limbs off her favorite dolls. Maggie had cried, but her father reminded her that Rebecca was only a tiny child and what did it matter about favorite dolls or broken windows or broken furniture. Rebecca was just a baby and Maggie was growing up and grown-ups were expected to tolerate the irresponsible actions of a baby sister. So Maggie tolerated Rebecca, but deep down inside she hated the spoiled little girl who was almost ten years younger than herself.

Yes, she hated her. It surprised her to admit it now without feeling guilty. But it was true. She hated Rebecca; she'd always hated her.

At first it was mere sibling jealousy, but that jealousy festered. In school Maggie had had no time for boyfriends and dating because Rebecca had to be looked after. And when Rebecca was old enough for boyfriends Maggie found she was too busy trying to keep Rebecca on an even keel to have time for her own male friends and admirers. Their parents fell ill just about then and Maggie worked to provide for them, and made sure Rebecca didn't become too wild.

Despite her efforts, however, Rebecca refused to behave; she just became wilder and more unmanageable in everything she did. Rebecca was spoiled rotten and Maggie had fallen into the trap and spoiled her as much as everyone else did even though she hated her.

Of course, she told herself she spoiled Rebecca because Rebecca was weak and needed to be spoiled. Maggie was strong and independent and could afford to spoil someone who could not look out for herself. She misinterpreted her responsibility as love for her sister, and when their parents died, Maggie became Rebecca's 'parent'.

Thank God for Rod. He was the one who made her see what true love was really like. Rod made her forget Rebecca and live for herself for a time. Even though it was Rebecca who brought her and Rod together originally, Maggie still hated her, but she was glad Rebecca thought Rod so dull and uninteresting. It gave Maggie the opportunity to call herself to Rod's attention.

After they fell in love and married, Rebecca decided that Rod wasn't all that boring a man after all. She set her cap for him again, and won him back. He succumbed to Rebecca's persuasions and charms.

Maggie would win him back again. True, Rod was weak, but it was because of his weakness that Maggie adored him. She felt she was strong enough for both of them. Regardless of what he'd done, she would forgive him for doing anything because she loved him more than life itself. She would overlook anything just to be back in his arms again.

She hugged herself and closed her eyes, thinking of Rod's strength, the passion in his kisses, the deep need he had for her.

A scream followed by a loud crashing noise brought her to her feet. It came from somewhere far at the back of the house. It had sounded like a woman's scream, but Maggie could not be certain. Had Rebecca come back? Or perhaps it was Rod. The thought that he might be back and might have fallen into trouble again made her forget fear or caution. She ran out of the room, toward the kitchen.

The kitchen was empty. Her eyes wandered over near the stove where she half-expected to see the limp, lifeless body of poor Sophie huddled on the floor. The events of that night seemed to be repeating themselves.

Maggie noticed that the cellar door was open. The bulb Mr. Babcock had replaced was burning.

'Rod,' she called softly. She felt no fear, no apprehension, just an eagerness to be in her husband's arms again. She was positive he was here; she could feel his presence now.

No answer. Not a sound.

He was here, though, Maggie told

herself. She could almost hear his breathing. It had to be Rod. Rebecca was with David.

'Rod. If you're here, answer me. Rebecca told me everything,' she lied. She hesitated for a moment, waiting anxiously for his voice. When it didn't come she started down the steps.

'Rod. It's Maggie. It's all right, darling. Please answer me.'

Maggie walked cautiously between the crates and barrels, peering to the right and to the left, searching behind anything large enough to conceal a person. She walked until she came face to face with the far wall — the wall that held the bricked-up doorway, the wall against which Heather Lambert's portrait had leaned these many years.

She gasped when she saw a figure lying under a pile of fallen bricks. 'Rod!' Maggie screamed as she raced toward the bricks and began throwing them off the half-buried body. When she saw the face she recoiled. It wasn't Rod's face.

'Mrs. Johnston!' Maggie exclaimed as she stared at the lifeless body.

Mrs. Johnston was dead. Maggie knew that before she touched the body. The head, a hand and part of an arm lay exposed in the rubble. Maggie felt for a pulse. She did not expect to find one and was not surprised when she didn't. She knelt there, staring at the body of Mrs. Johnston, not knowing what to make of it.

It was obvious that the bricked-up doorway had collapsed over her, killing her instantly. But what did it all mean? Why had Mrs. Johnston sneaked down here into the cellar and tried to break down the barricade of bricks? There were no answers to her questions. Mrs. Johnston was not alive, and it seemed she was the only one from whom Maggie could have sought answers.

Maggie stood up and backed away from Mrs. Johnston's body. She would have to report what had happened to the proper authorities. She glanced again at the lifeless form barely visible underneath the pile of bricks. Oddly enough she felt no terror in what lay before her eyes. By all rights she should be near hysteria over what had happened, but she was not. Another dead woman lay in front of her now, as Sophie had lain in front of her before, yet Maggie did not feel alarmed.

Two women had died within the span of a day or two. It was strange how cool and detached she felt about it. It was as if she were a disinterested observer of a tragedy that did not concern her. She felt apart from everything and yet she was in the dead center of what had happened.

Slowly she backed away, gazing down at Mrs. Johnston's dead body. Then her eyes wandered into the room that had been bricked up for so many long years. The light from the cellar made the inside of that room faintly visible. There was a strong, unpleasant odor emanating from its depths. She remembered Mr. Babcock mentioning the old cesspool. She would have to have the bricks put back.

As she stood there looking into the room, something caught her eye. There was something dark lying in the center of that foul-smelling room. She leaned forward and peered into the dimness. There on the floor lay the skeleton of a human being. A gasp caught in Maggie's throat. The skeleton was draped in a man's suit and the bones seemed to gleam in the darkness as though lit from within.

Maggie wondered who it could be. She glanced from the skeleton to Mrs. Johnston. The woman obviously knew there was a skeleton behind that brick barricade and was trying to reach it for some reason or other. Why? What had Mrs. Johnston to do with this long-since dead man? It had to have been a man, Maggie told herself. But who?

She mustered up her courage and stepped over the pile of bricks underneath which Mrs. Johnston lay in death. Maggie's hands were trembling slightly as she touched the moldering suit jacket that covered the upper torso of the skeleton, carefully keeping her eyes averted from the deep, blank holes that once had held eyes. There was no wallet, no means of identification, she found. But her search of the pockets was not completely unrewarding. In the inside pocket of the suit jacket her hand touched something crisp and old. She extracted a folded piece of paper. Maggie turned toward the light and carefully undid the folds. It was a letter.

★   ★   ★

Dearest,

I must talk with you. The doctors say Heather will recover. She should be home within the week. If you persist in staying with her I swear I will try again. Next time I will succeed. I love you too much to let you go. Take me away, please. I'll come tomorrow night. I can be there and return here before Heather misses me. I should arrive about nine o'clock.

Be there or I will not be responsible for what I do if you are not.

Edwina.

★   ★   ★

'Edwina?' Maggie mused. She knew no one named Edwina, yet she had heard the name somewhere before. Who was Edwina and who was this man?

She looked again at the skeleton. There

237

was a ring on the right hand. The ring, like the name Edwina, was familiar. It was a bit feminine for a man, she thought. She looked more closely at it. In the very center of the design Maggie saw the name 'Heather' engraved on a sprig of golden heather.

'Louis Lambert,' Maggie said as she stared at the ring. It was the very ring she'd seen in the portrait of Heather's husband, the one that was hanging on the living-room wall. She remembered David telling her that Heather had had that ring designed to look like a sprig of heather so that her husband could never forget her.

'So he did not run off and abandon her. He was here all the time. Poor Heather,' Maggie said with a sigh.

But Heather never knew he was here. The diary . . . Heather's diary. Heather believed her husband had left the house and her.

And Edwina? The name was in the diary; that was where she'd seen it.

She glanced again at the letter. 'Edwina,' she said as she let her eyes move toward the dead body of Mrs.

Johnston. Her mind began to click. Was Mrs. Johnston the author of this incriminating letter? She obviously knew of the existence of Louis Lambert's skeleton. Did she know also of the existence of this letter? Was that why she had tried to knock down the bricks — in order to recover this damning piece of evidence?

But why? Why now, after all these years?

Of course, Maggie thought suddenly. David had mentioned that the people from the state highway department had purchased the house and it was to be inspected and torn down eventually. In razing it the skeleton would certainly be found, as would be the letter. If Edwina had killed Louis Lambert and had hidden him behind that brick barricade, her crime would be discovered after all these years.

Things were beginning to make sense of a sort, Maggie thought . . . rather, things *would* make sense if Mrs. Johnston's name was Edwina.

She would have to find out. It shouldn't be difficult. Slowly she slipped out of the awful-smelling room, stepped over the pile of bricks and went across the cellar toward the stairs and the telephone in the hall above.

16

Rebecca sat huddled in the far corner of the front seat of the car. The wind was making a racket around them as David drove slowly, picking his way cautiously around the branches and other litter that was strewn on the road. The sky was black as pitch, like an overhanging shadow of doom.

'I don't know why you have to drive back to Pinebrook tonight,' Rebecca said. 'I wanted to stay in San Francisco for a few days.'

'Sorry, love. It can't be helped. Business first, you know.'

'Business,' Rebecca said with a sneer. 'Is that all you can think about? Besides, what possible business do you have to take care of this time of night?'

'I told you. I can't take any time off right now. I have that council meeting about the state land deal first thing in the morning.' He glanced at her out of the corner of his eye. 'As it is, I should not have taken today off. This deal is important. It means a lot to me.'

Rebecca continued to sulk. 'I suppose the deal is more important than me?'

David smiled tolerantly. 'Nothing is more important than you, Rebecca, but you must be sensible. We can't live on love, you know. I've got to make money.'

'I have money.'

'You won't have it long by the way you keep throwing it around.'

Rebecca gave him a cold look. 'Men. You're all alike.'

David continued his tolerant smile. 'Ah, but where would you be without us?'

Rebecca slumped lower in the seat. She stared out at the blustery night. A sign told her they were entering the town of Pinebrook.

'Pinebrook,' she said, almost to herself. She glanced over at David. 'How long is this business going to take tomorrow?'

David shrugged. 'Shouldn't take too long.'

'I hope you don't expect me to sit around that room of yours all day.'

'I said I didn't think it would take long.'

'Well,' Rebecca said, straightening in the seat, 'I'll take my car and drive back to San Francisco and wait for you there.' She fiddled with one of the several gold bracelets on her wrist. 'I hate this dumb town,' she said as they passed some of the outlying buildings.

'Well, I'm afraid you're stuck with it for a while at least,' David said.

Rebecca snapped her head around and scowled at him. 'I thought you said we'd live in San Francisco.'

David tightened his hands on the wheel. 'Not immediately,' he said. 'I can't just shut down the business and fly off like a bird.'

'Why not?'

'Rebecca, be sensible.' He shot her a quick glance. 'I said we'd live in San Francisco, but I thought you realized that I would have to make arrangements to sell the business and lay some plans for the future. That's why this council meeting tomorrow is so important. These guys from the state can be a great help to me in the future.'

'I have no intention of staying in

Pinebrook any longer than tonight. And if you love me as much as you say you do, you'll meet me in San Francisco after your stupid meeting tomorrow.'

'Rebecca, be sensible.'

Rebecca gave an exasperated sigh. 'And I thought you were going to be a barrel of laughs.'

David shook his head as he pulled the car up in front of Mrs. Johnston's house. 'I am, you must remember, a business man first. I have responsibilities.'

'Your first responsibility should be to me.'

He reached over and took her hand. 'Please, Rebecca,' he said patiently. 'You have got to understand that I can't just rush off half-cocked. I've got to see the council tomorrow and that's that.'

Rebecca pulled her hand away from his. 'Is it the council you have to see, or is it my sister?'

'Really, Rebecca. You're being childish.'

'Am I, David? You've been thinking about Maggie all day . . . you've mentioned her often enough.'

'The only time I mentioned Maggie

was when I told you I didn't think you should have run off like that without telling her. She'll be worried sick about you. You should at least telephone her.'

'I have nothing to say to my sister. And neither have you.'

To her surprise David laughed. 'Your jealousy is showing, my pet.'

She shot him an angry look. 'You bore me, David.'

He shrugged indifferently. 'So I bore you. Come on, let's go inside before we get blown away.' When Rebecca didn't make a move he said, 'Do I bore you too much for you to stay here with me tonight?'

She glowered at him for a moment but didn't speak. She'd made a mistake about David. He was just like Maggie, all stodgy and dull and straight as an arrow. How could she have thought herself in love with this small-town lothario? He had about as much spark as a wet log. What a fool she'd been to let herself get entangled with him.

Well, it wasn't too late to untangle herself. She'd made a mistake thinking

David was the man for her. Besides, she found out he wasn't as wealthy as he'd led her to believe. He was a fraud; he'd deceived her into thinking he had inherited a bundle. He was just a small, hick real-estate man. Sure he was just about the best-looking guy she'd ever seen, but looks were a dime a dozen. She could buy looks if she wanted just that in a man.

She got out of the car. 'I left a coat in your room,' she said. 'I'd like to get it. Then I intend to drive back to the city.'

'Tonight? Are you nuts?'

'No, I'm not nuts, David . . . very sensible. Isn't that what you said I should be, sensible?'

'You can't drive all the way back there tonight. This wind is treacherous. There's a storm brewing.'

'I've driven in worse weather.' She hurried up the walk and onto the porch. At the door she turned and waited for David to unlock it for her. When he did she hurried inside and started up the stark white staircase.

'Is that you, David?' Mr. Johnston

called from the living room.

David and Rebecca exchanged looks. 'Yes,' he called as he handed Rebecca the keys to his room. She hurried on up the stairs and left David to talk to Mr. Johnston.

'Hello, sir. Quite a wind blowing up outside.'

Mr. Johnston sat in his wheelchair in the doorway. He looked to be in a highly agitated state. He motioned quickly and wheeled himself back into the living room. David followed.

'Yes, David, it's pretty wild outside from what I can tell by sitting here at the window. It worries me. Mrs. Johnston's out there someplace. She should have been back a long time ago.' He fidgeted in his chair.

'Where did she go?'

Mr. Johnston turned and rolled his chair over to the window. 'She said she had some business that couldn't wait. She's been gone almost three hours.' He shook his head anxiously from side to side. 'I told her to forget it, but she wouldn't listen to me.'

David frowned. 'Forget what?' he asked.

'Some personal business,' he said softly. He lowered his head and let out a deep sigh. 'I'm afraid Edwina's in trouble.' He hesitated for a moment, then raised his head. He looked at David, studying him for a moment and then said, 'I need your help, David.'

'What kind of trouble do you think your wife's in?'

Mr. Johnston sat silently for a moment. Then, as if finally reaching a long and difficult decision, he said, 'She went to Heather House.'

'But why?'

Mr. Johnston started nervously lacing and unlacing his fingers. He shrugged, looking like a man who'd said something he suddenly regretted.

'I don't understand,' David said.

Mr. Johnston let out a long, deep sigh. 'I'm going to tell you something that I hope will remain a secret between us,' the old man said. 'You're the only one I can trust. You've lived here in Pinebrook all your life, many years of it in this house.

Your father and I were very close friends. I've looked upon you more or less as a son. You're a good man, David, a man of integrity, I know. I can't trust anybody else here. Their mouths are all like running brooks that never stop. But I've got to tell someone, someone who will help.'

'Of course you can trust me, sir. Whatever kind of trouble your wife has gotten into, I'll only be too happy to help if I can.'

'I never thought I'd ever tell anybody this, but you see, I'm worried sick about Edwina. I just know something's happened to her. I'd go to Heather House myself if it weren't for this blasted wheelchair.'

David saw the fear in his eyes, the quiver on his mouth. 'Calm yourself, Mr. Johnston. Surely your wife isn't in any kind of danger. Why don't I call Mrs. Garrison at Heather House? If your wife is there Maggie will know if she's all right or not.'

'Mrs. Garrison won't know if Edwina's there,' Mr. Johnston said sadly.

'I thought you said your wife went to Heather House?'

'Not on a social call. She intended stealing into the house without anyone seeing her.'

'I'm afraid I still don't understand, sir.'

Again Mr. Johnston sighed. He turned his back on David and stared out the window at the threatening night.

'If there is something in the house that she wants, I'm sure Mrs. Garrison has no objections to her removing whatever it is,' David said calmly, trying to ease Mr. Johnston's anguish.

'It isn't all that simple. I'm sorry, David, but I can't tell you what she went after. I ask only that you trust me and that you go to Heather House and bring Edwina home.'

'Of course I'll go,' David said, glancing toward the stairway, thinking about Rebecca. He put his hand on the old man's shoulder. 'Nothing has happened to Mrs. Johnston. Try not to worry. I'll drive out to the house right away.'

As he spoke he turned around, hearing Rebecca's footsteps on the stairs. He patted Mr. Johnston's shoulder again and started toward the hallway. Rebecca tried to brush past him.

When David told Rebecca he was going to Heather House, she was sure to suspect that it wasn't because he was interested in finding Edwina Johnston, but Maggie Garrison.

Let her think what she wishes, he told himself. There was something slightly unnerving about Rebecca. She was still the vivacious, tempting woman he'd met, but there was something else, something almost frightening about the things she said, the things she did, the way she acted.

'I'm leaving,' she said curtly and swept out the door, slamming it behind her. David just stared after her. He started to follow.

'David,' Mr. Johnston called.

David hesitated with his hand still on the doorknob, then he turned back. Let her go, he thought. She certainly wasn't the only desirable female in the world. He thought suddenly about Maggie.

'If you find Edwina and she is all right,

please don't mention that I sent you after her. She'd be upset with me. Just pretend you came to see Mrs. Garrison. If Edwina is not there, check the grove of trees at the back of the house. That's where Edwina parks the car. She doesn't want Mrs. Garrison knowing she's slipping into the house. If her car is there, then find some excuse to go down into the cellar.'

'The cellar?' David asked with surprise. 'But why?'

Mr. Johnston waved a nervous hand and looked away. 'Just trust me, David. I can't explain. What Edwina feels she must have is in the cellar. Just do as I ask. I wish I didn't have to ask this of you, but as you can see there is no one else and it is, of course, impossible for me to go myself. And after what happened to Sophie, I'm afraid.'

David frowned. 'What does Sophie's death have to do with your wife?'

David heard Rebecca start up her Mercedes and drive off.

'Edwina saw who killed Sophie. I'm afraid he might try to kill her, too.'

'*He?*'

252

'A man. She said he was a stranger to her, but she'd recognize him again if she saw him. She wasn't sure whether or not the man saw her hiding in the cellar doorway when it happened.' He glanced up at David. 'Now, you see why I'm so afraid for her? I'm certain something has happened.'

'But why didn't she go to the police?'

'Because . . . No, I can't tell you that. The police would only ask what Edwina was doing there in the first place. She could never tell them that and so she chose to remain silent. You see,' Mr. Johnston continued, 'the stranger — the man who killed Sophie — is still in Heather House. Edwina said he did not leave after hitting poor Sophie. He disappeared into the servant's wing. She is sure he is still there.'

'Still at Heather House?' David gasped.

Mr. Johnston nodded his head. 'Edwina said she got the impression that he'd been there for quite a while. She'd overheard snatches of a conversation between the man and Sophie just before the man hit her.'

'Good God!' David exclaimed. His eyes widened. 'Maggie,' he said suddenly.

He turned and rushed out of the house.

17

A hand reached out and grabbed Maggie's arm, pulling her around. She screamed, but when she saw him standing there in the shadows, her scream turned into a gasp of joy.

'Rod,' she said, almost inaudibly. 'Rod.' She threw herself at him. He tensed against her embrace. She felt his breath softly on her hair.

'Oh, Rod! I knew you weren't dead. I knew it!' she exclaimed as she tightened her arms around him and felt the tears begin to stream from her eyes.

The man stood straight and rigid, like a cold, marble pillar. 'Hello, Maggie,' he said flatly.

Maggie stiffened. The voice wasn't the voice she'd wanted so desperately to hear; it wasn't Rod's voice. She pushed herself back and through her happy tears she stared up into the shadowy face. Her eyes widened in amazement and shock.

'George!' she gasped. She let go of him and anxiously looked around, praying that Rod would be standing near Rebecca's supposedly dead husband.

'Aren't you surprised to see me, Maggie?' His voice was like ice cubes.

'Where's Rod?' Maggie demanded firmly. She felt suddenly frightened . . . afraid to hear his answer.

'Where do you think? At the bottom of the lake, of course.'

Maggie's hands flew to her mouth. She bit into her knuckles to keep back her scream. 'No,' she groaned. 'No.'

'Ah, but yes, Maggie dear. Your dim-witted husband has gone to his reward, as they say.'

'I don't believe you. He's alive. I know he's alive.' Again she looked around with frantic, anxious eyes.

'He's dead, Maggie. Hasn't my dear wife convinced you of that yet?'

'No, he's not dead,' Maggie insisted.

George nodded gravely. 'He is most definitely dead, Maggie. Take my word for it. After all, I should know; I was there, wasn't I?'

256

Maggie stared hard into his face. 'I don't believe you; I won't believe you.'

George shrugged. 'So don't believe me. It doesn't matter whether you believe me or not. You are so naive, Maggie,' he said, reaching out to put his hands on her shoulders. The look on his face made her cringe from him. 'Rebecca and I plotted the whole thing right under your noses and you never suspected a thing.'

'*You* and Rebecca? I thought . . . '

'You thought it was Rebecca and that stupid husband of yours,' he said, finishing her sentence for her. 'Oh, Maggie, surely you don't think Rebecca was interested in that lout? She only played up to Rod to make you jealous. She thought by keeping you occupied with trying to hold on to your dear husband, you wouldn't see what we were really after.'

Maggie took another step back, scowling at him.

'It was money, of course, that we wanted. That salary I made as an insurance salesman could never keep Rebecca and me content. No, my little wife and I have always had expensive tastes, as you know.'

'Rebecca hated you,' Maggie managed to say.

George threw back his head and laughed. 'Hated me? Hell, I'm the only man in the world capable of making Rebecca happy. We both wanted the same thing — money — and the only way to get it was to talk you and Rod into that big insurance policy. If you remember, we took one out at the same time. Oh, we gave it a lot of thought. First Rod and I would die,' he said. The ugly grin was plastered on his mouth. 'And then you, Maggie dear.'

Maggie groaned and took another step away from him. 'No.'

'But of course you must die. Surely you know that. Rebecca got my insurance money and you got Rod's. Well, we're not satisfied with just half the pie. We want all of it. You made Rebecca your beneficiary without giving it a second thought. That was a lucky break. Rebecca thought if she insisted she be named your beneficiary you might start being suspicious. You were always naive, but never stupid, I must admit. We knew you'd guess it all sooner or later. Thankfully it was later . . . but too much later,' he said.

Maggie just stood there speechless. Yes, she'd suspected, of course, but she'd guessed the wrong characters in the play. She knew Rebecca was behind some hideous scheme but she was sure it had been with Rod and not with this husband whom she had continually said she despised.

What a fool she'd been. When the insurance company mentioned the troubles George had had with the law, she should have been smart enough to guess that it was Rebecca and George. Her mind was in a jumble. Rebecca and George had been so convincing about how much they hated each other.

As though reading her thoughts, George said, 'Rebecca and I did a pretty good job convincing everybody that we hated each other. We had everybody fooled. We used to laugh about it when we were alone.'

Maggie, finding her voice at last, said, 'You can't get away with this, George. You and Rebecca will be found out.'

'How? Nobody questions the fact that I am legally dead. If you suddenly die in an accident — a fire, let's say — who's to know that there was dirty work behind it? Rebecca's off with that local real estate character, I suppose.' As an afterthought he said, 'She'll tire of that jerk in a week, if not before. She knows where the good times are. I don't mind her having an occasional fling. In the meantime, if she's in the city and your house burns down with you inside, or you have an accident of some kind, who's to suspect that Rebecca had a hand in it? Remember, Maggie, there isn't supposed to be anybody in this house but you.' He glanced over toward the far wall where Mrs. Johnston's body lay half-buried under the bricks. 'Who was that old lady?'

'Mrs. Johnston,' Maggie found herself saying. The name came out of its own accord. 'You killed her, too.'

George laughed. 'No, I didn't kill her. I guess I was responsible, though. She was trying to push down that bricked-up door. I bumped into something and the noise made her spin around. When she saw me she screamed and fell against the bricks. What was she doing here, anyway?'

Maggie thought about the skeleton of Louis Lambert. Would her skeleton lie next to his one day? It seemed years ago now that Mrs. Johnston had said the house was evil.

Maggie had refused to listen, but now, standing here in front of a man who meant to take her life, she wished she had listened. Why had she been so blind? Even now, regardless of the evidence standing before her, she refused to accept the fact that Rod was dead and she was marked to follow him. Rod couldn't be dead. He'd come back to her someday, just as George had come back to Rebecca. She must keep herself alive.

How could she flee from this menace in front of her?

Talk to him, she told herself. Talk. Play for time. Take his mind off what he intends doing to you. Talk, Maggie. Say something. Tell him anything, but keep his mind occupied until you can seize the opportunity to run.

'There's a skeleton behind that brick wall,' Maggie forced herself to say. She tried not to let her voice give away her intentions.

'A skeleton? Hey, I like that,' George laughed. 'This old barn is just stacked high with corpses. A regular Bluebeard's castle.'

Maggie turned slightly and took a step in the direction of where Mrs. Johnston's body lay. George followed closely. She stopped, standing beside a tall pile of crates and boxes. 'The woman lying there was trying, I think, to retrieve this letter from the dead man's skeleton.' She had the letter in her hand. Slowly she unfolded it and showed it to George.

Interested, he made the mistake of reaching for the letter. When he lowered his eyes to the writing Maggie yanked on the stack of boxes behind her and pulled them down on George's head.

George groaned in pain as the heavy boxes and crates toppled over him and he fell under their weight. Maggie turned and ran as fast as she could toward the stairs. She dashed up, tripping over the top two steps and banging her arm hard onto the floor. Pain shot up through her shoulder.

With a groan she staggered into the kitchen and slammed the door shut. There was no key in the lock. Hurriedly she pulled a kitchen chair over to the door and lodged it underneath the knob, but the floor was highly waxed and polished and she knew the chair would not hold. She heard George's footsteps coming fast up the cellar stairs. As she turned to run, the cellar door crashed open and George made a lunge for her.

Maggie screamed. She grabbed a kettle from the stove and flung it at his face. George ducked and the kettle went clanging across the floor. She snatched up a long, heavy poker that rested next to the old coal stove. She gripped it firmly and swung at George, driving him back from her.

George crouched before her, looking for an advantage.

'I killed one woman in this kitchen,' he sneered. 'It seems I'm in a rut by killing another in the same place.' He made a grab for her.

Maggie swung the poker. It connected with the upper part of his arm. It didn't seem to phase him, although it did cause him to step back out of range.

'You play rough, Maggie. Well, have your fun. It's the last you'll enjoy.' Again he made a lunge for her. This time she aimed the poker more carefully. She struck him on the side of the head. George yelped and staggered, and fell sideways onto the floor.

Maggie made a dash for the door. She was through it in a flash and racing as fast as she could for the telephone on the hall table. She was careful not to let go of the poker as she snatched up the receiver and frantically dialed for the operator. It seemed forever before she heard the woman's voice.

'This is Maggie Garrison at Heather House,' Maggie said in a rush. 'There's a man here. He's trying to kill me. Call the police.' She screamed and dropped the phone as George charged through the door, blood streaming down his cheek.

Maggie raised the poker and brought it down hard. It grazed his skull and

264

thudded hard into his shoulder. George nearly fell again but he stayed on his feet and made still another grab for her. Maggie found herself backed into a corner under the staircase.

'Stay away from me, George,' she said as she waved the poker menacingly at him. 'I don't want to hurt you any more than I have to. It isn't going to do any good to murder me now. The police know there is someone here trying to kill me. You won't get away with this.'

To her surprise George only smiled at her. 'I'm dead, Maggie. Remember? George Shepard, beloved husband of your dear sister, is dead . . . drowned . . .' He laughed. 'No one will suspect Rebecca because she's far away from here. I made sure of that. I told her to be sure she was with someone, someone who could testify that they were miles away from this mausoleum when you died. Let the police come. I'll be well on my way before they get here.' He made a sudden grab for the poker but Maggie was too quick for him and swung again, knocking him back away from her.

He stood there for a moment, searching her face. Then he said in a crooning voice, 'Your arms are getting tired aren't they, Maggie? Can't you feel it? Can't you feel that tiredness in your muscles from holding up that heavy poker? It's getting heavier and heavier, Maggie. You are not going to be able to hold onto it for much longer, are you? Already the muscles in your arms are beginning to tire under all that weight.' He made another quick grab for her but again she was too fast for him.

He was right, though. Her arms were beginning to grow numb, or at least she felt as though they were. The power of suggestion, she thought. She mustn't listen to him.

'The poker must weigh at least a hundred pounds, Maggie,' he crooned. 'It's getting heavier and heavier.' He took a step closer, keeping his eyes glued to hers. 'You'll have to put it down, Maggie. You can't hold it much longer. It's too heavy.'

The poker seemed to be gaining weight by the second.

Yet she could not let go of it. It was her only chance at saving her life. She had to hold on. She had to fight him off until the police arrived. To show she still had strength left in her arms she swung the poker again. It was suddenly heavier than ever and almost slipped from her grasp.

'I have no compunction about killing you as you killed poor Sophie,' Maggie said as she threatened him with the poker, refusing to look into his eyes.

'Stupid Sophie,' George said with a sneer as he continued to crouch and study her for an advantage. 'She knew I was here in the house all along, of course. I got here long before you and Rebecca. Sophie and I were old pals by the time you two arrived. Sophie used to call me Mr. Lambert. Yes, we had good old gab sessions in that kitchen. She was just as dim-witted as that husband of yours, Maggie.

'But like Rod, Sophie finally started to see the way things really were. Little did you know that I was in the kitchen when you and Rebecca and the boyfriend were having yourselves a gay old time in the other part of the house. Sophie was going to tell you that there was a man living in the servants' wing . . . a man she fed and looked after. Of course I couldn't let her tell you that. I had no other choice but to shut her up.'

'Murderer,' was all she could find to say.

George laughed again. 'Would you have called Rod a murderer if he were standing where I stand now? I think not, Maggie. You could overlook a little thing like murder in Rod, but not in me. Why, Maggie? Why am I so evil and Rod so forgivable? If he were in my place — if it had been he and Rebecca who cooked up this whole scheme — you'd still be willing to forgive and forget.'

Sudden guilt made Maggie cringe within herself. He was right, of course. Having suspected all along that it was Rod and Rebecca who arranged for George's death, she still would have found it in her heart to absolve Rod from blame. Here she stood, fighting for her life, prepared to kill as George had killed, and still wishing Rod was standing before her, murderer or not. She was no better than George and Rebecca. She would willingly have closed her eyes to Rod's mistakes, his terrible deeds, just to satisfy her own selfish desires for his love.

Her thoughts took her mind away from the threat of George Shepard. The poker wavered slightly for a second. In that split second George made a grab for it. He wrenched it out of her hand and threw it far behind him.

Maggie screamed as he reached for her throat.

18

Mr. Johnston sat at the window gazing out at the twisting trees, the scattering leaves swirling in the grasp of the angry winds. He heard David's car drive off down the street and he was alone again with his troubled thoughts.

Edwina *had* to be safe. Nothing must happen to her, he kept telling himself, yet he knew it would all be over soon. He was sure that Edwina was gone; he could sense it deep inside himself. She was together with Louis at last. It was where she had always wanted to be.

Heather Lambert had never suspected what was going on under her roof. Her husband and her sister, Louis and Edwina . . . and Heather never knew.

He tried not to think about that night, the night Edwina came running to him, her eyes on fire with fear and horror. He could still hear her voice sobbing, 'I've killed him. I've killed

Louis. Oh, help me. Please help me.'

He'd always known Edwina never loved him, Mr. Johnston told himself. She had loved only Louis Lambert and she killed him in a fit of rage . . . killed him because he told her he loved Heather's money more than Heather's poor sister, a sister who would inherit nothing because of a father who hated her. Heather had everything; Edwina had nothing.

Louis's death was an accident, of course, he told himself. Edwina hadn't meant to kill him. Her temper got out of hand. And when she confessed to the death of Louis Lambert she ran to him and said she'd marry him if he would help her.

'God forgive me,' Mr. Johnston sobbed. He shook his head. He loved Edwina too much to deny her anything and so he went with her back to Heather House and they bricked up Louis's body in the room where the old cesspool was. Heather was in the hospital at the time. Food poisoning, the doctors said it was. Mr. Johnston knew differently. Edwina had tried to get rid of Heather before she fought with Louis. Of course she never admitted that, but he knew she had. Edwina was desperately in love.

Then Heather came back and was told Louis had run off with a young girl. It was afterward that Edwina remembered the letter she'd written Louis, begging for him to meet her, to run away with her. With shock Edwina remembered that the letter she'd written him was in his pocket the night she murdered him. She forgot to remove it from that jacket pocket.

At the time it didn't matter. No one suspected foul play. Everyone knew Louis for what he was: corrupt, immoral, no good . . . Everyone was convinced he'd simply run off with another woman.

Mr. Johnston shook his head again. Edwina was always a clever woman. She left no clues. Even the bricked-up wall was explained away. She told Heather that while she was in the hospital there was an upheaval of the cesspool and Edwina had had it bricked up. Heather was too upset with Louis for having run off and never became suspicious.

Then they were married. Mr. Johnston

smiled, remembering how happy he'd been, even though Edwina never was happy. She learned to be in time, however, and he felt his life fulfilled.

When Heather died, Edwina again tried to fight for custody of her property, but she overlooked one little detail. By all rights, Louis Lambert was still supposedly alive and the house was his according to the law. Edwina could hardly prove he was dead so she decided to try to forget everything and they settled down to live out their lives.

Still, Edwina could not rest, knowing that even though Heather was dead, her portrait still reigned with Louis's over the house. Her pettiness grew until she coaxed her husband to go with her to Heather House and move the portrait to the cellar, propping it up against the brick barricade behind which Louis Lambert lay.

'I thought that was the end of it,' Mr. Johnston said to the empty room. Again he shook his head, remembering his wife's agitation when she had heard from David McCloud that Heather House was to be sold to the state and torn down. The town council managed the property in Louis's absence, but when the statute of limitations ran out they saw fit to sell it off at a handsome profit, still refusing to honor Edwina's claim to the property.

Edwina had to get the letter back before it was discovered. He remembered how heatedly they argued but she would not listen. She'd gone there with a low-powered explosive to try and dislodge the bricks; she said she'd weakened them but not sufficiently.

Then she saw Sophie's murder.

'It's over,' Mr. Johnston said. 'I know it is.' Tears began streaming down his face. He remembered having said those exact words once before . . . the day he lay in the hospital after his second stroke, convinced that Edwina would have nothing more to do with him now that he would be a cripple the rest of his life. But it hadn't been over then. Perhaps it wasn't over now, either.

'No. This time it is finished,' he said.

Well, let it be finished at last, he thought. With Edwina gone there was nothing to live for. She was dead. He knew that now. Something deep inside himself convinced him of that fact. She hadn't returned because she could not return. David would find a corpse in the cellar of Heather House. His wife was gone and he would never see her face again.

He sighed. Well, at least he would end up knowing that Edwina finally got what she had always wanted. She was with Louis Lambert. She was there with him now and he knew deep in his heart she would never come back.

The house suddenly seemed unbearable. The room seemed to close in on him. He was alone . . . truly alone . . . and would remain so forever.

He broke down and started to cry.

19

George hesitated when he heard a car drive up and stop in front of the house. That brief moment of hesitation gave Maggie her chance to escape. He turned his head in the direction of the sound. Maggie snatched the chair near the telephone table and banged it into his shins, doubling him over with a groan of pain. She raced by him, sprinting for the front door and whoever had come by car to rescue her.

Maggie flung open the door and started to rush out into the blustery night but her way was blocked. She froze, staring, then stepped back. Rebecca was standing menacingly before her. Before Maggie could think what to do, she found herself in George's iron grip.

'You won't get away this time, Maggie,' he growled. Then George looked at his wife. 'What in hell are you doing here? I told you to take lover boy to San

Francisco so you'd have an alibi.'

Rebecca ignored him. She brushed by them and went into the living room. 'You were supposed to have this all taken care of by this time,' she said.

George dragged Maggie with him as he followed Rebecca, kicking the door shut behind them. 'There were a few complications,' he said.

'Like what?'

'For one thing, there is some batty old dame lying dead in the cellar. She was digging in a brick wall.' He thought that funny and laughed.

Maggie continued to struggle.

'What are you talking about?' Rebecca asked impatiently. She went to the liquor cabinet and poured herself a drink.

'Some old bat sneaked down into the cellar just as I was getting ready to attend to your sister here. I went down to see what she was up to and she started hacking away at a brick wall down there. She saw me, got scared and fell against the damned thing and it collapsed on her. It banged her brains in.'

Rebecca stood holding her drink poised

near her lips. Her eyes moved to Maggie. 'Who is it?' she asked, seemingly blind to Maggie's predicament.

Maggie glared at her. 'Mrs. Johnston,' she spat and started trying to pull away again.

'What is she doing here?'

'You mean 'what *was* she doing here'?' her husband said with an ugly laugh. 'Maggie told me she was trying to get a letter away from a skeleton that's buried behind the bricks.'

Rebecca looked bored. 'Mrs. Johnston's dead?'

'As a doornail,' George said, sounding pleased with himself.

Rebecca downed her drink. There was a tiny frown at the bridge of her nose. 'A corpse in the cellar and one up here,' she said, glancing at Maggie, 'might complicate things.'

Maggie glowered at her. 'The police will be here shortly, which will complicate things all the more for you,' she said angrily.

Rebecca's eyes widened. She looked at her husband.

He gave her an apologetic look and turned his head to show her the gash on his cheek. 'She got to the phone before I could reach her. She whacked me on the side of the head with a poker and dazed me just long enough for her to call the operator and tell her who she was and that somebody was trying to kill her.'

Rebecca looked worried for a moment. Then her frown vanished and she smiled. 'Maybe it's just as well. You put Maggie in the car and get rid of her. I'll stay here and wait for the police. When they come I'll tell them the place was empty but that there's a body in the cellar. When they find Maggie in the car they will think she was trying to run away from Sophie's murderer and had a fatal accident. It will work out fine.' She glanced at her watch. 'You'd better get going, George.'

Maggie glared at her sister. 'I always knew there was a vicious streak in you, Rebecca, but I never thought you would stoop to this. It's cold-blooded murder. You'll be found out. You will spend the rest of your life in prison.'

Rebecca narrowed her eyes. 'At least I

won't have you whimpering and simpering around after me,' she said. 'At last I'll be rid of your sniveling, your complaining, your dull, boring lectures. I've waited a long time for this, Maggie. Too long. I've hated you ever since I can remember. Seeing you dead isn't going to turn a hair on my head, so save your breath. Nothing you can say will have any effect whatsoever on what is going to happen to you. We need your money as well as Rod's. When the insurance company hands it over I'll at last be able to live the way I have always wanted to live. And, best of all, I'll be free of you.'

'Don't you think the insurance people will become rather suspicious in view of the fact that you'll inherit George's money, Rod's money and now mine?'

'So let them get suspicious,' Rebecca said indifferently. 'They can't prove anything. I've been with David all day. George here is legally dead. We'll be careful until we have the money in hand and then they can do what they want. They'll never find us.'

'You silly, selfish, spoiled fool!' Maggie

yelled. 'I've always known what terrible things went on in that wicked mind of yours and I've always tried to protect you. Well, at last I, too, can say what I've thought all these years. I'll die happy just knowing you know what I've always thought of you. Has it ever dawned on you, Rebecca, that I've disliked you as much as you disliked me?' She watched Rebecca's expression remain unchanged. 'Yes, I've always despised you, but at least I felt a responsibility to you because you were, after all, my only sister, my only family. Loyalty is what it is called, but I doubt if you know the meaning of the word.'

Rebecca turned her back. She fixed herself another drink. 'You aren't telling me anything I didn't always know. I'm glad to see you have finally let yourself face the truth. I know you've always hated me. You're a fool, Maggie,' she said, turning to face her sister. 'You've always been a fool.' She glanced at her husband. 'Get her the hell out of my sight, George.'

'Come on, sister-in-law. Let's go.' He started to drag her toward the front door.

He stopped. 'No, we can't use your car, Rebecca. If they find Maggie in the Mercedes they'll know you two were together.'

'You're right,' Rebecca said as she frowned again. 'Wait a minute,' she said, brightening. 'The old gal in the cellar. Surely she must have come here in a car.'

'Yeah,' George said. 'I do remember hearing a car drive up and park at the back of the house.'

'Take that, then. They'll think Maggie borrowed it to make her escape.'

'Right.' He started to drag Maggie toward the kitchen.

For a moment she went with him without resistance. It seemed useless to struggle. George was going to kill her and there was nothing she could do about it; nor did she really want to do much. She was numb with shock and with shame.

She had been a fool. Worse than that, it was as if she had been haunted, possessed by Heather House. She looked back over her actions of the last few days and saw how much she had been influenced by the spirit of the dead Heather Lambert, following her direction rather than making her own. If she had not been so convinced that Rod was alive — had not waited for him as Heather had waited for Louis — she would have seen the truth sooner, and none of this would have happened.

'Don't try to move,' George warned her, letting her go for a moment. He had led her down into the cellar, and now he knelt beside the body of Mrs. Johnston, searching for car keys. He found them in the pocket of the coat she was wearing.

'Here they are,' he said, holding them up as if she should be pleased by the sight of them. 'Come on, let's go for that ride I promised you.'

He gave a wicked little chuckle and, seizing her arm again, pulled her up the stairs. Weakly, dazedly, Maggie went with him. For a moment, she thought she detected the scent of Heather.

20

Rebecca was standing in the kitchen as George and Maggie came up out of the cellar. The two sisters exchanged looks but neither of them spoke. Maggie thought that enough had been said already, and what hadn't been said should have been said years ago. She knew it was useless to plead with Rebecca for her life.

'I'll kill her somewhere along the road and leave her in the car,' George said.

'Won't that look suspicious?' Rebecca asked.

'No. She already told the telephone operator there was a man here trying to kill her. They'll think the same one that killed Mrs. Johnston killed her, too — which is right, after all. I'll double back here and wait till the police have come and gone.'

'That might be too dangerous,' Rebecca said. 'Better wait somewhere for me to pick you up. There's an old wooden bridge about three miles down the road. Hide there and wait for me to come and pick you up. I'll say that I can't bear to stay here after all that has happened, and then I'll come for you and we can drive into San Francisco. I'll flash my lights three times when I come.'

George nodded his agreement to this plan. 'Let's go,' he said to Maggie.

They went out toward the clump of trees at the back. As they entered the little grove, the moonlight revealed an antiquated Buick parked there. George opened the door on the passenger side and shoved Maggie inside. Then he came around and slid behind the wheel.

'I'm glad you've gotten smart and haven't tried any more tricks,' he said, fitting the key into the ignition. The motor roared to life. 'The best thing is for you to do what I want you to do.'

Why should I? The words suddenly flashed into Maggie's mind. Yes, she was doing exactly what George wanted her to do, cooperating in his efforts to kill her. She was being a fool again, giving up her life because Rebecca and George wanted her to.

Looking back, she could see how time and again she had sacrificed her life for others. She had lived her life for Rebecca, and later for Rod. More recently she had lived her life for an illusion, a dream that Rod was still alive and would come back to her.

Now she was again giving up her life, but this time it would be final. And suddenly she knew she did not want to; she wanted to live, wanted to live for herself for the first time. That was what Heather Lambert had tried to tell her, with that final whiff of heather. Heather was telling her not to make the same mistakes she had made.

But it's too late, she thought. George had turned the old car around expertly and was driving it onto the road. The headlights pierced the darkness, and they were on their way. There was no hope of escaping from George. They were going too fast for her to open the door and jump out, although she considered the idea.

Suddenly on the road ahead she saw another pair of headlights coming toward them. Perhaps it was the police. But what good would they do her now? They would arrive at Heather House to find her gone. Rebecca would entertain them with some very fine hysterics, telling them her sister was gone. And by the time they found her, Maggie would be dead, lying in an abandoned car, and everything would have worked out just the way George and Rebecca wanted it.

Unless . . . An idea crossed her mind. She watched the oncoming headlights, drawing rapidly nearer. The driver was driving fast, hurrying somewhere. They were almost abreast of the other car.

Suddenly, with no time left to consider her plan, Maggie leaned across the seat and seized the steering wheel. The action caught George off his guard and before he could stop her or tighten his grip she had given the wheel a violent yank. The car veered across the road, toward the oncoming headlights.

There was a scream of tires on pavement, followed by a collision and the ripping of metal against metal. Maggie was thrown against the dashboard, and her head struck the windshield, leaving her dazed.

For a moment there was an awesome silence. Then, from the direction of the car they had struck, a man's voice said angrily, 'What the hell's the big idea?'

It was David's voice — even in her daze Maggie recognized the sound.

'David,' she tried to call to him, struggling to get out of the car.

But George was still conscious, too, and he seized her wrist. 'Oh no,' he said, 'not without me.'

David had come up to the car. Looking in, he said, 'Maggie, is that you?'

'David,' Maggie started to say, but George interrupted her.

'Yes, it's her, pretty boy.' He suddenly produced a gun, and gestured threateningly with it. 'Back up, and don't try any tricks.'

'What is this?' David demanded, but he moved backward as George had ordered, allowing George and Maggie to scramble from the wrecked car.

'Shut up,' George said, walking around to look at the two cars. He saw that the car he was in had suffered a broken axle, and would be inoperable. But David's car had nothing worse than a few dents.

'I'll have to take your car, pretty boy,' he said, sneering at David. 'Let me think how I can work this.'

'Work what?' David wanted to know.

'You've just been elected as the man who's going to kill Maggie here.'

'Kill Maggie? You must be crazy!' David cried.

'Yes, David, he is crazy,' Maggie said. 'It's no use trying to argue with him.'

'Right you are,' George said. 'And I'm tired of hearing you talk, Maggie. I think the time has come to say goodbye.'

Instinctively, Maggie and David moved together, and he put an arm around her. George lifted the gun.

'Wait,' David said.

'For what?'

'For them,' David said. At that moment they were bathed in bright lights as a car screeched to a stop just beyond David's. They had been so engrossed in the tense scene that none of them had been aware of the approaching police car.

George turned, staring for a second into the blinding lights. He must have realized how obvious the scene was to the men getting out of the car, because he suddenly panicked. Turning, he ran wildly into the trees alongside the road.

'Stop or I'll shoot!' the policeman cried, but there was no response from George, only a distant crashing in the underbrush as he fled.

★   ★   ★

It was a nightmarish night — the trip back to the house with the police, the confrontation with Rebecca who, caught unprepared, blurted out the truth. Then it was necessary for Maggie to go back into town with David, to make a statement at police headquarters.

It was nearly morning by the time it was over and the policeman in charge told Maggie she could go. George still had not been found.

'Don't worry,' he assured Maggie, 'we'll find your brother-in-law. It's hard to hide around here.'

David had stayed with Maggie through-out the ordeal. Now he guided her gently back to his car.

'Come on, I'll take you Mrs. Johnston's,' he said, opening the door for her. 'You can have my apartment and I'll sleep in one of the spare rooms.'

'I can go back to Heather House,' she said.

'Not tonight. It wouldn't be safe with George still on the loose.'

'Yes, probably you're right. But I'll go back tomorrow.'

'Do you really want to — after everything that happened there?'

'It wasn't the house to blame,' she said. 'It was Rebecca and George. If anything, I think Heather may have saved my life.' She was remembering Rebecca as the policemen had taken her away. 'It was this damned house,' she said viciously. 'This house ruined everything.'

'Maggie, the house will be gone in a few months' time. And it is haunted, isn't it?'

'It was — but I think now that Heather will finally know peace. And there are things from the house I'd like to keep. Heather's portrait, for one.'

'I had in mind that the two of us could start a life together,' he said, looking deeply into her eyes. 'Without the burdens of the past.'

She smiled back at him. 'We needn't throw out the baby with the bathwater. Rebecca is gone. Much of my past is gone. But I'd like to have Heather with me, I think. I understand her, and I think she understood me. If I'd listened to her warnings . . . ' She let her voice trail off. For just a brief instant, she'd thought she once again caught a scent of heather.

Yes, Heather was at peace now. And so would she be, with David.

THE END

We do hope that you have enjoyed reading this large print book.

Did you know that all of our titles are available for purchase?

We publish a wide range of high quality large print books including:

Romances, Mysteries, Classics
General Fiction
Non Fiction and Westerns

Special interest titles available in large print are:

The Little Oxford Dictionary
Music Book, Song Book
Hymn Book, Service Book

Also available from us courtesy of Oxford University Press:

Young Readers' Dictionary
(large print edition)
Young Readers' Thesaurus
(large print edition)

For further information or a free brochure, please contact us at:
Ulverscroft Large Print Books Ltd.,
The Green, Bradgate Road, Anstey,
Leicester, LE7 7FU, England.
Tel: (00 44) **0116 236 4325**
Fax: (00 44) **0116 234 0205**

Other titles in the
Linford Mystery Library:

TWELVE HOURS TO DESTINY

Manning K. Robertson

At the height of the Cold War one of the most trusted and important British agents in Hong Kong, Chao Lin, suddenly vanishes, and in London Steve Carradine is put on the case. Now hints are filtering through to Hong Kong of a new weapon with which the Chinese hope to dominate the world, and Chao Lin is the only man outside of China to possess this vital information. Carradine's assignment is simple: Find Chao Lin, discover the nature of this secret weapon, and bring both out of China!

THE CON MAN

Gerald Verner

Elmer Myers has nursed Mammoth Pictures into becoming the second-largest picture-making corporation in Hollywood. But for the last three years, mysterious accidents have held up the completion of his films, until all the profits have been eaten up in overheads. Now Myers has borrowed heavily, staking everything on the making of an expensive super-epic to restore his fortunes. But when his film editor is murdered and the only negative of the completed film stolen, Myers realises he has a deadly enemy intent on his ruination . . .

PATTERN FOR SURVIVAL

Manning K. Robertson

Dr. Villiers is one of the country's leading missile research scientists. When he disappears, the alarmed British Intelligence are quick to send in their top agent to investigate. Steve Carradine is able to recover the scientist before Russian agents can smuggle him out of the country, but the affair turns out to be part of an even larger conspiracy . . . And unless Carradine can penetrate to the heart of the mystery and take out the mastermind behind it, the safety of the entire western world is in jeopardy!

BLOOD ON THE DRAGON

Norman Firth

A mysterious murder cult . . . a man who has no identity . . . an ancient hidden temple in the remote hills of China . . . And mixed with these ingredients is the brutal story of the Purple Dragon Tong and the man who knows too much . . . While in *Sinister Honeymoon,* two newlyweds have their celebrations interrupted by a vampire! Can they find a way to escape the perils they face before it's too late? Two stories of murder, mystery and the supernatural by Norman Firth.

MISTER BIG

Gerald Verner

Behind all the large-scale crimes of recent years, the police believe there is an organising genius. The name by which this mysterious personality has become familiar to the press, the police and the underworld is Mister Big. When murder and kidnapping are added to his crimes, Superintendent Budd of Scotland Yard becomes actively involved. Eventually the master detective uncovers a witness who has actually observed and recognised Mister Big leaving the scene of a murder — but before he can tell Budd whom he has seen, he is himself murdered!